Love *in the* New Year

Lisa Farmer

Names: Farmer, Lisa, 1970- author.
Title: Love in the new year / Lisa Farmer.
Identifiers: ISBN: 978-1-960505-42-2 | LCCN: 2023910738
Subjects: LCSH: Dance teachers--Fiction. | Parents of autis-
    tic children--Fiction. | Single mothers-- Fiction. |
    Work and family--Fiction. | Music teachers--Fiction. |
    Man-woman relationships-- Fiction. | LCGFT: Ro-
    mance fiction.
Classification: LCC: PS3606.A72 L68 2023 | DDC: 813/.6--
    dc23

Dedication

To my son, my miracle, my joy.

To my sister, who is always there.

Love in the New Year

Chapter One

"Five, six, seven, eight, prep, plié, pirouette, lift, *port de bras*, and finish. Nice job, everyone! Thank you, and Happy New Year! See you next week!"

Leah Preston beamed at her young students as they packed up their dance bags. She opened the door to the dance studio, waving to all the eager parents who waited for their little stars.

Though the wooden floor of the studio was scratched from wear and creaked from age, Leah was grateful for the space her long-time friend, Debbie Irwin, rented to her at an affordable price. When Debbie's husband had decided to retire from his business ten years prior, he hadn't sold the property. Rather, he and Debbie had graciously transformed the building into a dance studio with a small office, along with an upstairs two-bedroom apartment, for Leah and her son, JJ.

As Leah grabbed her coat from the office, she looked into the empty studio. She closed her eyes, remembering where she had been a little more than a decade ago, before the dance studio was in existence. Then, the image of herself holding JJ as a newborn came to her mind, and Leah's heart filled with joy. She opened her eyes and smiled at the worn dance floor, the ballet barre, and the mirror stained with tiny fingerprints. Her dance studio. For the past few years, and into that new year, she greeted each day with contentment and gratitude.

JJ and I have come a long way, she thought and nodded in satisfaction.

Leah zipped her coat, turned off the stereo system and lights, then headed down the street to pick up JJ from his music class. She glanced back at the red sign above the door, Dance World, and proudly breathed it in.

Dance World stood amidst residential homes on a willow tree-lined street, with a public playground in its center. JJ loved the playground, especially the baseball field that was adjacent to it.

The New England winter brought a brisk whip to the wind, with a frigid, dewy scent in the air that promised snow. Leah shivered and pulled her scarf up over her nose. *Thank goodness*, she thought, *Bridge of Music is just a short walk.*

To divert her attention from the wintry nip, Leah visualized the spring season. The high school baseball team held practices and games at the field by the playground. Leah and JJ were frequent spectators and would sit on the bleachers close to home plate; according to JJ, that was the best view. JJ, with his jovial spirit, was always animated in his commentary. Often, he'd call the pitch even before the umpire would. JJ would also make sure that everyone nearby knew the score, and he was always quick to cheer for the home team.

Along the border of the field, past the outfield, there sloped a hill, which was a popular spot for the children, including JJ, when it was carpeted with winter's white blanket. As Leah walked past the hill and the field, she imagined the joyful sound of JJ's laughter as he went flying down the thickly frosted hill on his sled.

Around the corner sat the quaint Main Street village of the cozy town in Massachusetts. Bridge of Music had been a mainstay in the village for more than forty years. Highly revered by residents, it was a wonderful place of inclusion for those with or without disabilities to learn, play, and grow through music. The staff were certified music therapists, speech and language pathologists, and occupational therapists, and the studio offered private instrument lessons, vocal lessons, and group music for all ages. JJ participated in the group music sessions, a structured social group which used various toys and used musical instruments to play and share. The group also listened to a variety of musical genres to practice calming strategies.

As Leah stepped inside Bridge of Music, she inhaled the warmth within and rubbed her gloved hands together, in an effort to defrost the chill in her bones. The waiting area was quite occupied, though relatively quiet, with parents, caregivers, and a few small cherubs awaiting the arrival of the children from music group or individual lessons. Leah waved to a few of the parents as she headed toward the check-in desk.

"Hi, Leah! JJ's just about done," Nicole Waterford, the tall, bubbly office manager informed her warmly from behind the desk.

"Hi! How are the girls today?" Leah asked. She and Nicole had grown up together in that small town, the neighborhoods of their youth within walking distance of one another and only a car's ride away from the Main Street village. In their early years, if they hadn't been at each other's childhood homes, they could've often been found on Main Street, strolling through the shops. The close bond of their friendship had continued to that day, with the added delight of their children's rapport.

Nicole's twins were in high school, a few years older than JJ's eleven. Sometimes, when they weren't otherwise busy with after-school activities, the girls sat for Leah and played with JJ. Leah was always grateful for their kindness and patience with her son, whose enthusiasm was evident every time he was with the girls.

"Couldn't be more different, as you know." Nicole glowed with pride. "Lori's at home, glued to her computer coding video games, and Rebecca is at drama rehearsal, helping to create all the costumes."

Leah sat to wait for JJ. "Tell them to text me if they have any time soon to hang out with JJ. I'll order their favorite pepperoni extra-cheese pizza."

"I'll let them know." Nicole then answered the ringing phone with a smile in her voice. "Good evening, Bridge of Music! How may I help you?"

As the door to the music room opened, cheerful young voices filled the waiting area.

"Mommy!" With his arms held high, a toothy grin, and eyes that gleamed, JJ skipped over to Leah for a big hug.

"Hi, sweet face," she said, "how was music class?"

"Amazing!" JJ jumped up and down.

"I'm so glad! Say thank you to Ms. Lydia."

"Thank you, Ms. Lydia!" JJ repeated.

"You're so welcome, JJ." Lydia smiled at him, then lifted her eyes. "Leah, a moment please? I just wanted to let you know that, starting next week, a new therapist will be taking over my classes, Eric Hynes. He's highly qualified. All of the students know, and I'll be shadowing to make sure they all transition comfortably. I want to have more time to enjoy my grandchildren."

"Oh." Leah was worried. Lydia Fineberg, a mature woman with endless wisdom, was the owner and director of Bridge of Music and had known JJ since he was a baby.

"JJ will be fine, and I'll still be around." Lydia placed a reassuring hand on Leah's shoulder.

"Yes, of course. I'm very happy for you!" Leah hugged Lydia.

On their walk home, Leah wrapped an arm around JJ's shoulders for warmth from the winter chill and for comfort from her own uneasiness. Lydia was not only an exceptional music therapist, but she had also seen Leah and JJ through many hurdles over the years. JJ was extremely fond of Lydia, and her music class had become a steady constant in his routine. Changes in routine caused challenges for JJ, and having a new therapist as lead teacher in music class would be a significant disruption.

Chapter Two

Sunday morning brought with it a glistening sheet of eight inches of snow. Roads and driveways were cleared, the whirs from the snowplows echoing in the silence of the storm's aftermath. Houses became decorated with snow-people on their lawns, young children inspired to play in and create with the fluffy white canvas. High schoolers came out in abundance with shovels, looking to help neighbors and earn a little cash.

Leah and JJ spent an entertaining afternoon on the hill at the playground with their neighborhood friends. Children on sleds of a multitude of colors and sizes raced down the hill, then strenuously climbed back up, only to instantly glide to the bottom again. JJ preferred to play off to the side, away from the crowd. Leah nudged his sled and he held on during the ride, glee in his laughter.

By the time Monday morning rolled around, the snow stacks were piled high, the overhead view was a vast, solemn gray, and the bitter bite of the air seeped through coats. However, school was open as usual, thanks to the proficiency of the town's Department of Public Works snow removal team. Most of Leah's young students expressed their sadness to her. They'd been hoping for a "no school" day, so they could sleep in and play. JJ was very happy, though. With

JJ's autism, expected routines were a comfort, and for him, a "no school" day could sometimes be upsetting.

While Leah taught classes throughout the week, JJ either put on his headphones and played video games in the office of the dance studio, or he stayed upstairs in their apartment. Leah always made sure she looked in on JJ and had moments with him, here and there, between her classes.

She was grateful for the family and friends who helped her and JJ out with understanding and compassion. A few of her dependable, talented, and trustworthy high school students were kindly available to take over classes for her whenever she needed to attend to JJ, and she repaid them with free lessons.

It was important to her that JJ was involved in activities outside of school, and it warmed her heart to see him participate. His school team, therapists and activities instructors were supportive of both JJ and Leah, and she was grateful for her village.

"Today after school, JJ, at music class, there will be a new teacher, Mr. Eric," Leah reminded JJ. She looked into his eyes, trying to gauge his feelings.

"I know, Mommy," he replied. "Ms. Lydia told us, and she'll be there too. Hugs!"

JJ opened his arms. Relieved, Leah hugged him close. JJ was well prepared. *Everything will be fine*, she thought. She glanced at JJ over her shoulder. He put a spoonful of cereal in his mouth, humming a random tune, then stopped eating and stared off to one side. He continued to hum and, additionally, began rocking his body rhythmically in his chair. JJ often displayed those traits when he was nervous, bored, or overstimulated. Leah handed him the bubble-popper fidget toy to help redirect his focus to his cereal. As she turned back to the counter and packed his school lunch, she furrowed her brows and worry crept back in.

At least, she thought, *I hope everything will be fine.*

After her ballet class wrapped up, Leah walked a bit more quickly than usual to Bridge of Music. Drop off went fine, because

Lydia was there to open the door for JJ and the other children as they walked into the music room. Lydia's familiar face, with her long gray hair neatly twisted into a bun as it always was, allowed all the children to transition in easily.

"Hi, Nicole," Leah said as she unwrapped her scarf. "How have the classes been going with the new therapist? Have you met him?"

"Yes, I have," Nicole stated matter-of-factly, "and he's very impressive. He carries his guitar around with him, and he sings. His awareness and quick understanding of each individual child has allowed them all a very smooth and positive transition so far. And, of course, it helps that he's extremely…"

Nicole was cut off as Lydia opened the door to the music room. The children came out smiling, clapping, and excited as they found their parents. Leah craned her neck, wondering where JJ was.

"Handsome," Nicole whispered quickly and quietly in Leah's ear.

"What?" Leah turned to Nicole with a confused, worried expression on her face.

"Mommy, Mr. Eric is amazing! Hugs!"

JJ's ambitious embrace almost caused her to lose her balance; he was nearly as tall as Leah. Before she could stumble, two strong hands clasped her shoulders, steadying her. Leah lifted her head and looked up into the blue-gray eyes gleaming back at her. The man removed his hands from her shoulders and took a step back. Then, his smile, surrounded by a short, well-groomed beard with a hint of silver, widened, and he extended his hand.

"I'm Eric Hynes," he said. "JJ is a delight! It's a pleasure to meet you, Mrs.…"

Continuing to embrace JJ, Leah slowly raised her hand. "Ah…Preston. Ms. Preston. Leah." She breathed the words, feeling a warmth flow through her.

Eric held her hand and, rather than shaking it, cupped her fingers in his, letting his thumb dance across the top of her hand.

"Let's go, Mommy!" JJ tugged on Leah's coat. Eric released her hand, ruffled JJ's brown, wavy hair, and turned back toward the music room.

Leah let out a deep breath, not realizing that it had been caught in her chest. She stared at the closed door to the music room, still riveted by the most incredible eyes she had ever seen and the unfamiliar shimmering sensation she felt in her core.

When JJ tugged on her coat again, she blinked away her daze, then smiled at him. "Okay, sweetie." With another glance at the closed door, it dawned on her that she had forgotten to ask Mr. Hynes how JJ had done in class. She was relieved that JJ appeared to be calm and content.

As Leah and JJ walked out, Nicole raised an eyebrow at Lydia, who nodded a smile in response.

* * *

The following morning, after Leah dropped JJ off at school, she drove to the local YMCA and registered him for the next session of Special Olympics swimming. The Y had a heated indoor pool, which made for a great winter activity. She signed the waiver at the front desk, and as she turned toward the door, she collided with someone who was also headed out of the building.

"Ooh! I'm so sorry about that," she apologized. A whiff of freshly-scented soap wafted by her, indicating that the Y's shower had been recently utilized. Then, she noticed the face under the hoodie.

"No worries." The man flashed a smile and an amused chuckle.

"Oh, Mr. Hynes. Good morning." Leah smoothed out her coat and straightened her back. Eric Hynes was dressed in sweats, with his hands in his pockets and the hood of his sweatshirt pulled over his head, black locks of hair messed across his forehead. She noticed there were hints of silver at his temples, as well. "Did you have a good workout?"

"Pleasure to see you again, and please, call me Eric. Yeah, the gym is pretty good here. I was about to get a coffee. Care to join me? Leah, right?" he asked, though he already knew he was right. "We can discuss JJ and any concerns you may have. It always helps me to get to know the parents of my clients."

"Oh, okay. Coffee sounds good, thank you." Leah didn't have anywhere else to be, so she cautiously accepted, taking the opportunity to learn more about JJ's new therapist. "Have you been to Jenny's yet? Best café for breakfast and lunch in the area. Best coffee, too."

"Not yet. Sounds perfect. Lead the way."

As Eric opened the door for Leah, a whoosh of cold air blew across their faces and into the building. Leah tightened the scarf around her neck, pulled her hat over her ears, and tucked her hands into her warm, fleece gloves.

The early morning scene beyond was dark and overcast with thick, low-hanging clouds that almost appeared to be within reach. Snow stacks and store fronts illuminated the gray morning with splashes of color, and the bite in the air was dry enough to sting the eyes. Accustomed to the New England winter, people were out and about on the sidewalks in spite of the chill. As he stepped out into the elements, Eric turned toward the parking lot.

"Do you mind walking?" Leah requested. "It's just up this way." She pointed to her right. "Parking on the street is hard to find, and leaving our cars here would be easier." Eric nodded and walked beside her.

"I didn't get a chance, yesterday, to ask you how JJ did in class," Leah continued. "He seemed as though he enjoyed it."

"He did really well," Eric said. "He was a little timid initially, but once I began singing, he quickly lightened up. He didn't want to assist with tuning my guitar, but that's fine. He watched what the others were doing. His smile and laugh are contagious!"

"Yes, he definitely has that effect! Thanks for letting me know. I'm glad he made the transition relatively well. Changes in routine are challenging for him."

"I could see that, though I'm confident that he'll adjust to this new routine and will make progress."

"That's good to hear. Thank you." Eric's warm smile reassured her, and Leah released some of her worry. "How are you liking our little town?" she asked.

"So far, so good. Everyone is very friendly, and the kids I've met are wonderful." He slowed his pace to keep in stride with her. "I actually grew up just a couple of towns over from here."

"Really?" Leah was surprised to hear this.

"Yeah, it's been a long time since I've been back. I'm staying there with my younger brother and his very pregnant wife," he explained.

"Congratulations! You're about to be an uncle!" She clapped her gloved hands under her chin.

"Yeah, can't wait to meet the little guy." He smiled with anticipation.

"We're just about there. This unit here, Kay's Canines, is my sister's place. Kay and her wife, Stefanie, are dog groomers and trainers. Jenny's is the next one over."

"It's nice that you and JJ have family close by." Eric opened the door to the café for Leah. Although it was bustling inside, they were seated quickly at a window table.

Taking off her coat and hat, Leah's ponytail swayed just below her shoulders, brown with subtle red undertones, depending on how the light hit. She smoothed out the strands of hair that had become staticky from her hat. Her feminine frame was covered in black yoga pants and a black sweatshirt, "Dance World" written delicately across the chest in red. Leah's smile warmed her unpainted ivory cheeks, and her hazel eyes sparkled with golden specks.

Eric unzipped his fleece hoodie, lowered the hood from his head, and brushed his hair off his forehead. He wore a gray t-shirt, which highlighted not only the hue of his eyes, but also his broad, toned torso.

Leah took a deep breath, locked her hands on the table, and sat up straight. "So, Mr. Hynes, may I ask what your field of specialty is at Bridge of Music?"

Eric chuckled at her professional demeanor, and placed a hand over hers. "Yes, you may, but first must I ask you, Leah, to please call me Eric."

She relaxed her body, though his hand remained on hers. "Eric, what's your field of specialty?"

He moved his hand to his lap, and replied, "Speech and language. I've always been fascinated by cultural language and the ways in which communication can shorten the distance between those who would otherwise be unable to connect. Even as a kid, my nose was always in a book. I studied, received my MA and CCC-SLP from Northwestern in Illinois, went on to shadow in hospitals and private practices in Chicago, then kept climbing and found my first paying opportunity in San Diego, working with clients of varying ages and abilities. I connected well with the pediatric clients and made them my focus for many years."

Eric paused. While he was passionate about his profession, he knew not to assume others would be so interested. Leah intently listened to him, though was it only out of interest on her son's behalf or could she be curious to hear more about him?

The server came by with coffee and took their order. The smooth, vibrant fragrance of the coffee swirled up from their steaming mugs, filling the atmosphere. Leah added a cream packet to hers and circled her hands around the mug. Akin to a cozy fireplace, the beverage's warmth melted the chill in her fingers and nose. She closed her eyes as she brought the mug to her lips, blissfully savoring a sip of the creamy brew. Leah then brought her attention back to Eric, who sat back with his elbows on the arms of the chair and an amused smile on his face. She set her mug on the table and looked at him shyly through lowered lashes, then folded her hands in her lap and pivoted back to the conversation.

"Very strong credentials, Mr....Eric," she said. "What's your connection to music and, if you don't mind my asking, what brought you back here after your travels across the United States?"

He leaned forward, wrapping his hands around his own hot mug. "Well, my parents wanted us to be well-rounded, so they put us in sports and music lessons at an early age. My brother took better to the sports. While I enjoyed them, I'm much better at watching than I am at playing."

Leah smiled and let out a quiet laugh at that one. Eric continued, "Language is melodic. I took guitar and voice lessons for many years, as well as online music therapy courses from Berklee in Boston. I've found that the music and language combination really resonates with the kids I've worked with. Seeing the moments when they shine is why I do what I do."

Suddenly, Leah became misty-eyed and sat back in her chair.

"I get it." She blinked to clear her eyes. "Professionally and personally, I get it. It's nice to talk to someone who also understands." She sat forward again and fell, for one silent moment, into the sparkling blue pool of his irises.

Her emotional reaction moved Eric in a way he was unaccustomed to. Over the years, he had worked with numerous families, whose children's impairments had ranged from high-functioning to severe. Each parent had their own emotional story to tell, and he always listened and sympathized; he'd even become close to a few of those families and was humbled by their lifestyle and their children's bravery. Eric couldn't put a finger on why Leah's response stirred him, but he was intrigued to find out more about her and her son.

As they held each other's gaze, the server stopped at the table with their meals. Neither of them noticed.

"Sorry for interrupting. I don't know what came over me there." Leah laughed lightly and brushed a few strands of hair away from her eyes. She took a sip of coffee to heal her dry throat, then sliced her blueberry muffin in half. "I think you were about to say what brought you back here?"

"I've been doing most of the talking so far," said Eric, "but I'd be interested to hear more about you and JJ. I'm in the process of reading the kids' IEPs and have already finished reading through JJ's, but I know that's only a part of who they are." He scooped up some eggs and potatoes. "I'm sure you're quite familiar with JJ's legal IEP document qualifying him for special education and therapeutic services."

"Yes, I work closely with JJ's educational team and therapists. The goals, accommodations, modifications, and services of his IEP are all appropriate to support his individual needs and success, but it's very true that he's more than his IEP," Leah agreed. "Raising a child with a disability is extremely challenging and exhausting. I've had to do a lot of researching and learning, not just about autism, but about JJ's autism specifically. I've had to learn how to accept help, which is also hard, but I'm beyond grateful and try to find ways to give back. I do my best so that he can be his best, and he's come a long way. He's a whiz at math, enjoys watching sports, and playing video games. He's my miracle and my light, and he spreads joy to everyone!" Leah finished with an expression of pride.

"You're a devoted mom, Leah. Seems to me that both of you are very fortunate to have each other," Eric acknowledged. "JJ was very intrigued by my guitar. He stood next to me while I was playing it, and he kept humming."

"Yeah, he does hum a lot. Sometimes it's random melodies, and other times he hums songs he knows. I've tried to get him to take singing lessons, but he keeps telling me that he can't sing in front of other people."

Eric thought for a minute. "What if I come to your residence?"

"Excuse me?" Leah was taken aback, knitting her brows and tilting her head.

"If we schedule a time for me to bring my guitar to your place, where JJ is likely at his most comfortable, maybe that would give him the confidence to try singing with me? I'd start by having him just listen to me play and sing, and he could join in only if he wants to. It could be a start?" Eric offered.

"That's very generous of you, Eric, and it does sound like it could be good for JJ, but I can't afford private lessons," Leah responded. She contemplated the idea of him in her home; she and JJ had only just met him. However, Eric did seem to be a very intelligent, educated man with years of experience in pediatric disabilities, and Leah knew that Lydia wouldn't have hired him without a thorough background check. She could see that he understood and had compassion for the children he worked with. *Admirable qualities*, she thought.

"I'm offering," Eric countered, "and I'll discuss this with Lydia today. I have experience providing therapy services and music instruction in a home setting. A few SLP friends of mine, as well as a couple of music therapists I'm acquainted with, provide both home- and clinic-based therapy services. If it doesn't work out for JJ, then it'll just have been a one-time deal, no harm done."

"And if it does work out?" Leah asked.

"Then wouldn't that be wonderful for JJ! I'm sure we could figure something out regarding payment, at that time." Eric tried to sound convincing, though he knew that he wouldn't accept money from her. "How about Friday evening, after my sessions? Let's say, seven-fifteen?" he suggested.

Difficult as it was to push finances aside, Leah decided to take the opportunity for JJ. As much as she didn't want to admit it, she found there to be an undeniable charm about Eric. "Okay, Friday at seven-fifteen, but I insist on covering breakfast."

"Deal." Eric admired her determination and knew the cost of the meal would be relatively manageable. "Let me put my number in your phone. If JJ decides he doesn't want to do this, you can text me." He typed in his number while Leah paid the bill.

Since the weekend's snowfall, the sky had yet to clear, and the temperature remained below freezing. Therefore, not much melting had happened. However, the midmorning breeze carried less of a bite than its earlier counterpart, and the clouds had lifted their dull curtain. The sun was due out that afternoon, which would soften the snow stacks, followed by streams in the streets of slush around tires and boots.

Leah and Eric began to walk back to their cars at the YMCA. "So, not to sound forward, but what's your address?" Eric inquired.

Leah hesitated and took a step back, and Eric turned to look at her.

"For JJ, so I can work with him on Friday."

"Right, yes, for JJ." She tapped her hand to her head and picked up the pace. "I own Dance World, across from the playground. JJ and I live above the studio."

"Ah, got it, I've driven by there. I noticed Dance World written on your sweatshirt. Do you dance? Teach? Both?"

They passed the window of Kay's Canines. Leah waved at Stef through the window, who widened her eyes and pointed at Leah, then Eric, then back to Leah. Leah shook her finger laughingly at Stef and continued walking.

"I've been dancing since I was very little. I danced professionally for a few years at Disney World in Florida, mostly parades and stage shows at Magic Kingdom. I adore my memories from that time. Disney will always be special to me. JJ loves Disney too, though he hasn't been there yet. The music, the stories, the magic..." She held her hands over her heart, pausing for a moment of remembrance. "Anyway, injuries caused me to change course and want to come back home. I did some freelance teaching for several years, and now I own and direct my studio. I continue to teach, but I no longer perform. I've passed the performance torch on to my talented dancers." She looked up at him with a confident, content smile.

"That's a very accomplished journey, Leah."

"Thank you!" She curtsied with a bounce. They were almost back at the Y. "Okay, so that's JJ and me in a nutshell. Your turn. What brought you back here?" Leah wasn't sure why she needed to know this.

"For the past few years, I've been in Europe, lecturing, consulting, collecting data. Absolutely fascinating work, and it paid very well. Experiencing different languages and cultures… I thoroughly enjoyed every minute, though I did miss working directly with the kids. When I saw Lydia's online advertisement for the open position, I decided it was time for a new adventure."

Leah noted that he was looking for an adventure and filed that information away in the back of her mind, trying not to think about it. "Wow, that sounds so exciting! I've only traveled to Florida. What countries did you visit, and which was your favorite?"

"England, Italy, Sweden, France, and Ireland, and they were all my favorite. They're all so unique within themselves that they can't be compared," Eric recalled fondly.

They reached Leah's car in the parking lot of the Y. She leaned her back against the driver's side door. "I've always wanted to visit France, maybe because ballet terminology is primarily French. I've also been drawn the most to art by Degas and Monet. Maybe someday I'll visit France. Are you fluent in all those languages?"

"I learned a lot, read a lot. In England and Ireland I fared well, since the primary language is English. I know some, but not all, of their dialects. I can somewhat hold a conversation in Italian, French, and Swedish, but I'm definitely not fluent."

Eric took in her intrigued eyes, the subtle sideways curve of her smile. At Leah's home, he intended to focus on JJ's needs and goals. At that moment, however, it was only her, him, and a cool breeze. He placed a hand against the car, leaned in closer to her, and gently tucked the wisps of hair that were flying from under her hat behind her ear, uttering softly and melodically, "*Arbres enneigés.*"

Leah slowly closed her eyes, parting her lips. She could feel Eric's breath on her cheek, and when he spoke, it was as if she was being wrapped in a warm blanket and surrounded by a song. Her head leaned into his touch, his fingers lingering.

"What did you say?" she whispered, her eyes still closed.

"'Snow-capped trees,' in French," he translated quietly, while he caressed her cheek.

"What?" Leah opened her eyes, the same dazed and confused expression on her face as when he had first laid eyes on her in the music studio.

Eric smiled, amused, then tilted his head and repeated clearly, "'Snow-capped trees,' in French."

Leah looked in that direction and found that the trees behind the parking lot still had snow atop their branches. Scrunching her face humorously, she playfully pushed him back. Though inside, she wasn't quite yet recovered. "Ha ha, very funny."

"I'm glad you bumped into me this morning, Leah," Eric mused, as he put his hands in his pockets.

"Actually, you bumped into me." Leah lifted her chin, trying to defend her stance.

Eric laughed and turned away, walking toward his car. With a wave over his shoulder, he called, "Bye, Leah."

To the back of his hoodie, she tried to project, "Bye, Eric!"

* * *

Leah spent the remainder of the morning and into the early afternoon in the small office of her dance studio going through bills and student dues. Balances remained in the black, and she sighed with relief, though some months were a bit tight. *Hopefully*, Leah thought, *the upcoming winter concert will bring some new student enrollments.*

For the past several years, the town had sponsored the winter concert at the high school auditorium on the first Saturday afternoon in February. The high school and middle school jazz bands, orchestras, and choruses performed. Several students represented Bridge of Music, and accommodations were in place for them. Leah's dance team made a stage appearance, as did the local karate studio. Local artists, crafters, and bakers set up tables in the school's hallway and lobby, where they showcased and sold their works and goods. The town's mission was to support and promote local vendors, as well as to help those in need. Advertised through social media, the concert was usually well-attended by both the locals and those from surrounding towns, and all proceeds went to local area food pantries. Leah always passed out brochures for Dance World at the event and made herself available to speak to anyone interested in dance classes.

Leah's phone chimed; Kay was calling in for a video chat. "Hey! What's going on?" she answered, greeting her.

"So, Stef tells me that you were having a thing with a tall guy this morning and didn't bring him inside here," Kay said, seeking confirmation.

"First of all, I told her there was no thing. I shook my finger!"

"She says there's no thing!" Kay turned her head away and shouted to Stef, then looked back at Leah.

A muffled shout returned from Stef. "It's a thing!"

Kay shrugged her shoulders and rolled her eyes in the direction of the muffled shout, then turned her attention back to Leah. "She says it's a thing."

Leah laughed at her sister's antics, listening to the dogs howling in the background, "Second of all, he's JJ's new speech therapist and music teacher and is new in town. We just happened to both be at the Y and decided to have a quick bite at Jenny's." Leah waved her hand casually. "But I didn't want to overwhelm him with the craziness that is you and Stef, and I say that with nothing but love!"

"Ah-ha!" Kay's eyes widened. "So it *is* a thing." She again shouted to Stef, "You're right, it's a thing!"

The dogs howled a response first, then Stef. "What have I been saying? It's a thing."

Leah tried to change the subject. "I think your doggie customers are offended by all the shouting!"

"Nah, they're used to it. Happens all the time. They're just agreeing with us." Kay winked at Leah, then her expression became serious. "You know, I understand why you've been so guarded all these years, but it would be good for you to open your heart."

"JJ already has my heart."

"And he always will. But there can also be room for...a thing. After all, it's a new year. Be open to new possibilities," Kay concluded.

Leah smiled. "Love you."

"Love you." Kay ended the call.

Leah put the phone down and stared into the empty dance studio, no longer able to focus on paperwork. Every time she looked into JJ's ice blue eyes, she was reminded of his father. Because of JJ, she would never forget Daniel, the love she had thought they shared, or the fact that he had chosen to leave her before JJ was born. She had long since closed the door on her hurt and anger and had made peace with it. She had to, for JJ.

Leah knew what love really meant because of her son and had convinced herself that she didn't need anything else because her heart was already full. JJ was her priority, and his happiness was hers. Allowing someone else into her heart held a high risk. Not only could she be hurt again, but now, so could JJ. Leah had been doing just fine for many years...but had Eric opened up a part of her she had thought was gone?

Was Kay right?

* * *

Lydia walked into the music room and found Eric cross-legged on the floor, his guitar in his lap and IEP papers scattered on the floor around him like a rainbow.

"Excuse me, Eric," she said, "but I just wanted to make sure you're all set for sessions this afternoon. Do you have any questions about anything or anyone?"

"Thanks, Lydia. I think I'm good for right now."

"Great. Angie's mom called to say that Angie has a new wheelchair, but is struggling with maneuvering it. She's wondering if, this afternoon, you could help Angie to find strategies to more effectively cope and learn?"

"Got it," Eric replied. "I can help her to create a musical phrase or poem to match the new features of the wheelchair. That should make it easier for her to remember."

"Thank you, Eric." Lydia turned to head out of the room.

"No problem," he paused, "I ran into Leah this morning."

"I'm listening." Lydia came back in, grabbed a chair, and sat down.

"She mentioned that JJ seems too nervous to try singing lessons here in the studio, so I offered to go to her place to work with him. Of course, this won't take away from any of my sessions scheduled here."

"Therapies and classes have always been in-house here, not in the field," Lydia explained. "You have my attention, though. Tell me your thought process on this."

Eric presented his case. "JJ was attached to my hip when I was playing the guitar, and Leah thinks he could have musical potential. My thinking is that I can build his confidence by starting in the place he's most comfortable. His home."

"Interesting." Lydia crossed one arm over her leg, the other tucked under her chin. She looked around the room while she ruminated on what Eric proposed. The music room was the largest room in the two-floor building and was used for the group classes JJ was currently enrolled in. At the moment, the instruments were all tidied up in bins ready for students to explore, the mats rolled in a corner, and the chairs lined around the room. An elevator and a staircase led to the sound-proof lesson rooms on the second floor, which were used for individual vocal or instrument lessons and therapies. Lydia knew that JJ struggled with novel changes and that he associated Bridge of Music only with his class in the music room.

Eric tuned his guitar while Lydia was deep in thought.

"I have to say, Eric, it's not a bad idea. However, let's make the goal to be that JJ will eventually come here to continue voice lessons. While fieldwork is an additional positive bridge to the studio, it would involve hiring additional staff for field clinicians, as well as a new payment schedule. I want Bridge of Music to continue to flourish here even after I'm gone, where those of all abilities can gather for awareness, acceptance, and inclusion."

"Absolutely," he replied, "I completely understand. I figured I'd test the waters on a trial basis first, with no commitment, let JJ lead. If this proves successful, I'm more than happy to help you incorporate the necessary aspects into the program, and I'll let Leah know about this plan. Thank you for allowing me to try."

"How did Leah accept this? Did she offer to pay you?" Lydia inquired.

"She agrees that it could be a good opportunity for JJ, and I told her that we could figure out payment later, only if it works out. I don't intend for her to pay me, though," Eric answered honestly.

"This is where a payment schedule will be required. Leah will need to approve a fee increase for in-house lessons," said Lydia. "Here's a little tip about Leah. She's seen a lot in life, which is her story to tell you if and when she's ready. She is proud, stronger than she thinks, and will not accept something for nothing." She shook a stern finger.

"Duly noted," Eric promised.

Lydia smiled warmly, tapped Eric's shoulder and walked out of the room, leaving him alone in the stillness, left to ponder.

Chapter Three

*A*nother busy week, Leah sighed contentedly.

She pretended to be growing flowers with her littlest ballet dancers, listened to all the stories that her young students were always so excited to share, and worked on technique, along with performance skills, with her older students. She attended JJ's swim lesson with his Special Olympics team, clapping proudly when JJ swam a full lap in the pool. She helped him with homework and even played his favorite video game with him, *Mario Kart*, though she was not at all good at it.

Thursday evening, Leah and JJ picked up dinner at the local grocery store. The deli offered a decent selection of hot, prepared foods, and JJ chose his favorite: rotisserie chicken and mashed potatoes. Leah added to the basket some mixed vegetables for herself and sliced melons for JJ.

Once home, Leah prepared their plates, then sat down at the table with JJ.

"Ew, vegetables." JJ scrunched his nose and covered his eyes.

"They're yummy!" Leah said in a singsong voice.

"Chicken is yummy," her son replied, as he chomped into a wing.

Leah laughed as chicken ended up all over his hands and face. "JJ, tomorrow night, around seven-fifteen, we will have a visitor."

"Who?" JJ continued to eat without looking up.

"Mr. Eric from music class, and he's bringing his guitar."

"I liked when he played guitar, but why is he coming here?"

"He wants to play for you again. Would you like that?"

JJ looked up at Leah with apprehension. "Will you be here, Mommy?"

"Of course, if you want me to be."

"Yes. You can sit with me, Mommy, on the couch, and Mr. Eric can sit over there." JJ pointed towards the recliner chair across from the couch in the living room. A narrow open hallway connected the living room to the kitchen.

"Sounds good!" Leah said. "Now, finish eating."

"I love you, Mommy."

"I love you, my sweet face."

While they ate, JJ detailed his school day for Leah. She was relieved to hear that he had sat with a friend during lunch. She was always comforted to know how effectively the school staff supported him, as well as how accepted he was by fellow peers.

After dinner, while JJ was in the shower, Leah texted Eric to let him know that JJ wanted to see him on Friday, but seemed a bit nervous. Eric replied with a text that thanked her for the heads-up.

* * *

Leah no longer taught on Saturdays because she wanted the full weekend to spend with JJ; instead, her staff of high schoolers took over the Saturday classes. They were also part of her dance team, which had been featured in the annual dance recital and had performed at various other events. By late afternoon on Friday, the dance team gathered at the studio and rehearsed for the town's winter concert.

Eric parked his car in the lot behind Dance World, swung his guitar case over his shoulder, then walked up to the front entrance. He heard the music resonating from inside, a lovely instrumental version of "Music of the Night" from *Phantom of the Opera*. He entered what he assumed was the waiting area, though it was empty. Folding chairs lined one wall, while hooks for coats lined the other. Most of the hooks were occupied with coats and scarves, some hung neatly, others barely hanging on. The artwork on the walls depicted ballet dancers in different costumes and poses, pointe shoes with musical instruments, and sentiments about dance. One in particular caught his eye—"Passion Ignites the Dance from Feeling the Beat of the Music."

As Eric quietly opened the door to the studio, the crescendo of "Music of the Night" filled the room, shooting through him. He stood in the doorway, immediately captured by the movement. Dancers jumped high, dropped to the floor, stood to an extension, spun slowly and elegantly, all with incredible power and grace. They were all dressed alike in black dance pants and black tank tops sporting the Dance World logo, which helped to unify the choreography. Front and center, Leah, like a conductor with her orchestra, gracefully connected the dancers to their movements. Her back was to them, but she watched them through the full-length mirror. Just as the dancers seemingly posed to finish, "Music of the Night" turned into "Climb Every Mountain" from *The Sound of Music*, without skipping a beat. Eric enjoyed that instrumental piece as well and was impressed by the blending of music and choreography. The crescendo of "Climb Every Mountain" showcased three dancers *en pointe*. Each spun across the room, one at a time, with increasing levels of speed, serving as a very poetic ending to the dance. While the dancers held their final pose and the room became quiet, Eric started to clap.

The dancers and Leah hadn't noticed him, as he was somewhat hidden in the doorway at the back corner of the room. The dancers giggled, and Leah quickly turned her attention to where the sound came from. She saw Eric leaning back against the doorframe, right leg bent so that his foot rested on the door, his guitar over his left shoulder. After reasoning to herself that the shimmering tingle she felt inside her was due to being startled, she looked at the clock. *Seven-ten, he's punctual*, she noted.

"Excellent job, everyone! Again, from the top, without me this time." Leah walked toward Eric and cued the music with the remote she held. She looked just as she had the other day, though she had donned a Dance World t-shirt, with her sweatshirt tied around her waist.

"That was incredible!" Eric complimented.

"Aww, thank you."

"Did you choreograph it?"

"I did, and they're bringing it to life!" She motioned toward the dancers. "This will be their last run-through. We had to reschedule to today, because too many of them were at a gymnastics meet yesterday. Let me make sure they all have rides outside, then we can head upstairs."

"I'm honored I was able to see this. Is JJ upstairs alone?"

"Yes," she replied, "but as he gets older, he's become better about occupying himself safely, and I check on him in between classes. Sometimes he has a sitter, too. I think it would be best for me to go in first, then bring him to you at the door, since he's a little nervous."

"You're the boss." Eric mimicked a salute in acceptance of her wishes.

She motioned for him to step into the waiting area so the dancers could exit. Parents were already waiting inside, as Leah's rule was for no dancer to leave the building without a trusted adult.

Leah turned the music off. "Thank you, everyone! See you next week. Remember, the donation drive is a week from Sunday." Each dancer said goodbye to Leah, grabbed their belongings, and filed out. She locked the door behind the last family and closed down the studio.

"We can go up the back way," Leah said. She led Eric to the door at the opposite end of the studio, which opened into a hallway and stairs to her apartment.

Carefully, Leah unlocked the door and quietly stepped inside her apartment. She gestured for Eric to step in and wait, as she closed the door behind him. The entryway sported a coat rack and a rubber mat for boots and shoes. Leah took off her dance shoes and walked around the corner to the left, into the living room.

She found JJ standing in the middle of the room, playing *Mario Kart*. With the remote in his hands, he tilted it to correspond with the angles of the fast-moving track on the TV screen.

"Yeah, first place! I did the shortcut!" he exclaimed. "Did you see that, Mommy?"

"Yes, sweetie. That was a cool jump over the river!" Leah walked over to him and picked up the TV remotes. "JJ, we need to turn everything off now, because it's time to visit with Mr. Eric."

"Is he here now?"

"Yes, he's at the door. Come with me to say 'hi.'"

From the entryway, Eric heard the hint of nervousness in JJ's voice and the calming tone of Leah's. He hung his coat on the rack, placed his boots on the mat, then picked his guitar case back up. As they rounded the corner to greet him, Eric noticed that JJ looked down at his hands, fidgeting with a bubble-popper toy.

"Hi, Eric. How are you?" Leah modeled a welcoming greeting.

"Great, thanks. It's nice to see you again. Hi, JJ!" Eric kept an upbeat tone in his voice and tried to make eye contact with JJ.

"Hi." JJ did not look up.

"Let's all go into the living room." Leah turned JJ around and Eric followed. JJ plopped onto the couch and Leah sat down next to him, while Eric swung his guitar case off his shoulder and moved to sit on JJ's other side.

"No!" JJ yelled, pointing to the recliner. "Over there!"

Before Leah had a chance to intervene, Eric stepped in. "It probably feels a little unexpected to see me here," he said. "I understand that, JJ. But I don't understand where you would like me to sit. Please tell me in nice, calm words."

"On the recliner." JJ still did not look up.

"Sure. Thanks, JJ, for telling me nicely." Eric sat on the recliner, put the case on the floor, unzipped it, and took out his guitar. He had owned his Fender Parlor mahogany acoustic for a long time, since his days in San Diego, where he'd purchased it at a guitar store in the city. Of course, it had been restrung and refinished over the years, but its musical quality was timeless. He ran his hands across the wood with pride.

As Eric strapped the guitar around his back and began to tune it, he signaled for Leah to sit back casually. She did so and JJ snuggled into her, continuing to look down and fidget with the popper.

"JJ, do you want to help me tune the guitar?" Eric asked.

"No."

"That's fine." Once Eric was finished with the tuning, he began to strum melodic chords. Then, he started with the children's classic, "Twinkle Twinkle Little Star," though he embellished the melody of the chords on the guitar, as well as in the way he sang it. He continued with other popular children's tunes and included "Take Me Out to the Ballgame," as he remembered that JJ liked sports.

Music and song filled the room, with an uplifting cheer that floated, bounced off one wall, then another, and back again. Leah was awed by Eric's unique arrangements of classic songs, which brought out a grand, buttery sound from his guitar and an endearing rasp from his voice. Even though JJ was still focused on his fidget, he relaxed against Leah and she knew he had a listening ear.

Eric remembered that JJ enjoyed Disney music, so he started to sing "When You Wish Upon a Star," and JJ began to hum along. Eric caught and held Leah's gaze in elation.

"You've Got a Friend In Me," JJ requested for the next song.

"Ah, *Toy Story*. That's a good one, JJ!" Eric switched to playing fingerstyle rather than strumming with a pick, and a full, rich sound emanated from the guitar.

JJ put the fidget down. As he stood up and walked over to Eric, he said, "You can go now, Mommy." Then, he hummed along while Eric sang.

As much as Leah wanted to stay and watch JJ, she knew she had to allow him independence, especially when he advocated for himself. She decided to go into the kitchen to start dinner. *At least I can hear this magical milestone*, she thought. Quietly, she took out a small pot and a large pot, filling the large pot with water and setting it on a burner to boil. In the small pot, she poured tomato sauce, added some seasoning, threw in diced red and green peppers, then set it on another burner to simmer.

After a couple more Disney songs, Eric decided to challenge JJ. "Okay, JJ, now we're going to play a game. It's called 'make a match.' I'm going to sing a note, then you're going to try to match my sound. Here we go." Eric purposely did not give JJ a chance to object, plucking the middle C note on the guitar and singing it at the same time. "*Aahh*. Okay, JJ, your turn. Make a match!"

He played the middle C note again. In a soft voice, JJ echoed, "*Aahh*."

"Great job, buddy! A little higher this time—*aahh*. Make a match!"

JJ mimicked softly, "*Aahh*."

"Excellent! Here's a little trick. We're going to take a deep belly-breath, then when we let the breath out, we'll sing the note. Let's go back to the first note." Eric played middle C again. "Deep breath in…"

Together, they inhaled, and that time, JJ looked at Eric. They exhaled and simultaneously sang, "*Aahh*."

"You made a match, JJ, and your voice was as loud as mine! Guess what?" Eric asked with excited animation.

"What?" JJ laughed.

"You just sang your first note with me!"

"Yay!" JJ jumped up and down.

In the kitchen, Leah wiped away happy tears. JJ ran in. "Mommy!" he cried. "I sang! I'm amazing!"

"I'm so proud of you!" Leah hugged JJ, then looked up at Eric, who had come in after him, and mouthed, *Thank you.*

Eric smiled and winked in reply.

"Okay, hug over. I'm hungry." JJ broke away from Leah's embrace and sat down in his usual chair at the wooden table made for four. "Mr. Eric, you can sit here." JJ looked at Eric and pointed to the chair on his left, since Leah always sat to his right.

"Oh, JJ, Eric probably already ate dinner." Because of Leah's teaching schedule, she and JJ usually ate dinner later than what was considered a typical dinnertime. "You're certainly welcome to stay, though. There's plenty of pasta." Leah offered.

"Actually, I haven't eaten yet, and this smells quite good. Thank you both." Eric sat to JJ's left.

While Leah prepared another place setting, Eric turned to JJ. "Thank you for letting me come into your home," he said. "Do you feel comfortable with me here?"

"Yes." JJ bounced on his chair and flailed his arms.

"That's great! What does—"

"No, it's amazing!" JJ interrupted.

"I felt like saying great, but amazing works too." Eric acknowledged JJ, and tried to expand his vocabulary at the same time. "What does home mean to you, JJ?"

Eric's hope was to build JJ's confidence further through focused expressions of JJ's comfort zone. Then, he would have more tools to work with to foster JJ's growth. What he hadn't anticipated, though, were the responses that followed.

"Mommy!" JJ pointed to Leah as she served the pasta, put a bowl of salad on the table, and placed one piece of carrot on his plate. "I love Mommy and hugs and food. But I do not like carrots." JJ moved the small piece off his plate and onto the placemat.

29

"Aww, I love you too." She sat and opened her arms. JJ scooted his chair over and snuggled into her.

"What does home mean to you, Mommy?" JJ tilted his head up to look at her.

"Well, of course you." She gave him a squeeze. "But home, to me, also means a place where there is always love, laughter, and someone there, for all the amazing and happy, for all the sad and angry, for all the fun and easy, for all the really hard. Someone is always there, who wants to stay." For a brief moment, her eyes became lost in thought.

"I want to stay, Mommy."

"So do I."

They held their embrace for another silent moment, then JJ scooted his chair back over to his spot and looked at Eric. "What does home mean to you, Mr. Eric?"

Eric's fork slipped out of his fingers and made a loud *clank* as it hit the plate. He had been so stunned by the tender moment he had just witnessed that he hadn't realized he'd been staring at them, his fork dangling aimlessly from his grasp.

"Um." He ran a hand through his hair. "Well, JJ...I'm actually not sure, myself, but you and your mom...said it all." He quickly shoveled some pasta in his mouth.

So, the worldly speech therapist appeared to be flustered and, well, speechless, Leah merrily thought. The corners of her mouth slowly turned up into a delighted grin. Though part of her wondered why he couldn't answer the question, she found it appealing that his charming demeanor had become a bit unsteady.

JJ laughed. "You're funny, Mr. Eric."

Eric looked up and saw the humor in their faces, tabled his introspection, and laughed along with them. Dinner continued with lighthearted discussions about Boston sports teams, as well as all things *Mario Kart.*

After dinner, while JJ was in the shower, Eric helped Leah with the dishes. "Thanks again for dinner. It was very good."

"You're welcome. It's the least I could do," Leah replied. "Thank you very much, not only for helping JJ make a breakthrough, but also for humoring him when he went on and on about his video games. You don't have to clear the table. I've got it."

"I know you do." Eric smiled at her while he brought the plates to the sink. "I greatly enjoyed the company, and I had a lot of fun with JJ too." Eric leaned his back against the sink, while Leah loaded the dishwasher.

And the undeniable charm has returned, Leah thought, as she looked over her shoulder at him with a shy smile. Her eyes quickly fluttered, and the shimmering tingle ran through her again.

Eric shifted his weight, sliding his hands into the pockets of his pants. "In all seriousness, though, JJ made great progress tonight. His pitch and tone are quite good. I want to let you know that I spoke to Lydia about him." He recapped the conversation he had with Lydia.

Leah finished loading the dishwasher and washed her hands, while she listened to what Eric and Lydia had talked about. She also noticed that the shower had turned off, and heard JJ humming and making random sounds.

"That's great that Lydia thinks this could work out for JJ, as well as be beneficial to expanding her business," she said. "Her prices are fair, so I should be able to budget in the increase. Thank you for letting me know. How do you think we should proceed with JJ?"

"I'd like at least one more visit with him here, maybe two. Then, I believe we can transition him to Bridge of Music. Are you and JJ available this Sunday afternoon for me to come here? In addition, what sort of availability do you have to bring him to me during the week?"

"This Sunday afternoon is fine, though next Sunday we already have a commitment. As far as during the week, hmm." She crossed her arms and tapped a finger to her chin. "We could make two-thirty to three o'clock work on Mondays or Fridays, possibly on Wednesdays."

Eric took out his phone and pulled up his schedule. "Okay, this Monday two-thirty to three, I'm putting it in for me to come here. Let's see how he does before we schedule more. For Sunday, how's one o'clock?"

"Sounds good to both." Leah also added to her schedule on her phone.

Eric tucked his phone back in his pocket. "I remember you said something to your dancers about a donation drive?"

"Yes, that's my commitment next Sunday. I host a drive at my studio once every season, to collect certain gently-used or new items. The members of my dance team help me out, along with their parents. We have several bins in the studio to separate the items. Clothing, footwear, toys, and diapers go to local family shelters, while blankets and pillows go to local animal shelters. I advertise on my website and the town also posts it, so we usually get a good amount of donations."

"How extremely kind and honorable of you, Leah."

"It's just my way of trying to give back." Leah shrugged her shoulders. "I received an incredible amount of help in my time of need when JJ was a baby, and I'm fortunate to continue to receive help. So, I want to try to help others who are in need."

He had questions as to why she had been in need, but he remembered Lydia's advice; he didn't want to push Leah, though he was even more fascinated by her. "I would very much like to help out however I can. I'll let my brother, Ben, and his wife, Madelyn, know as well."

"Great, thanks! Donations can be dropped off between noon and two."

"We'll be there. I'd also like to help out with the drive itself. I can help set up and load bins, and Ben has a truck I can borrow to help with deliveries, or wherever you could use the assistance. Does JJ help?"

"Thank you, but that's really not necessary," she said. "My dance team and their parents help with all of that. JJ helps me go through his clothes that no longer fit and toys he no longer plays with, to see if any can be donated. Sometimes, though, it can be tough for him to give up his things. During the drive, Kay and Stef will be with him."

"I understand. If anything changes, please call or text me, anytime. I'm close by." He gently picked up her hands and cupped her fingers in his.

Leah saw the genuineness in his eyes. "Okay, I…I should go check on JJ. He'll want to say bye to you before you go," she said quietly. Though her body pulled her closer to him, her guarded heart pulled her further away. Leah slipped her hands out of his and turned toward JJ's room.

JJ was still in the bathroom, distracted by his fingers. "JJ," she said, "let's get lotion on those dry fingers, then you need to get your pajamas on and say bye to Mr. Eric."

"Can he play with me first?"

"Not tonight, it's getting late now. Would you like to do more singing with him another time?" She helped JJ to finish up while they talked.

"Okay, and then he can play?"

"Maybe. He's planning to come here on Sunday at one. Does that sound good?"

"Okay." JJ yawned.

Finally finished, they went back into the kitchen, though Eric wasn't there. Leah saw him in the living room, packing up his guitar. She guided JJ to the living room.

"You look comfortable, JJ. Ready for bed?" Eric asked, as he stood up and swung his guitar over his shoulder.

"Yeah, I'm tired." JJ yawned again.

"Tell Mr. Eric thank you," Leah prompted.

"Thank you."

Eric ruffled JJ's hair, which was still a little wet. "Have a good sleep, buddy."

JJ went off to his room, while Leah walked downstairs with Eric to the back door of the building. "Thanks again, Eric. I really appreciate what you're doing for JJ. See you Sunday."

"Yes, you will." With a striking smile and brightly-flowing waves in his eyes, he walked out the door. Leah locked it after him, leaned against the door, and closed her eyes, as the image of him remained in her mind.

Chapter Four

Eric whistled and drummed on the counter, pulling out a mug for coffee. The weather had brightened, and he was feeling just as sunny as it was outside.

"Well, someone's in a good mood. But keep it down, man. If you wake Madelyn up, she'll have my head!" Ben, of similar height and physique to his brother, though ten years younger, warned Eric, as he, too, reached for a coffee mug.

"I would enjoy seeing her try." Eric grabbed the coffee pot before Ben had a chance to.

"I bet you would. Seriously though, why are you so cheery at eight in the morning on a Saturday?"

"Sun's out and life is good, little bro." Eric gave Ben a pat on the back.

The flush of the toilet echoed through the walls and Ben cradled his head in his hands. "Now you did it." He threw his hands up and feigned a punch to Eric's chest.

A very petite, though very round, figure waddled into the kitchen. "What's all the noise?" Madelyn stared down both men, arms crossed on top of her bulge.

"Morning, sunshine!" Eric greeted Madelyn with a smile over his coffee mug.

Madelyn frowned her brows and looked at Ben, who shrugged his shoulders, then pointed to himself and shook his head. She looked back at Eric. "'Morning sunshine,' yourself. How's work been going?"

"Great! Met some awesome kids, friendly parents. Lydia, the owner, is a very wise woman, and it feels good to be working with kids again." He poured cereal into a bowl, then offered it to her. She held up a hand, so he added sliced bananas and milk for himself.

"Okay, and?" she prodded, while Ben leaned his elbows on the island and rested his hands under his chin. He was relieved that it was his brother's head his wife was going after. He watched with intrigue as her detective skills went into play.

"Oh, that reminds me, a week from tomorrow there's a donation drive. So if you have any clothes, shoes, blankets, or the like that you no longer use, then I'll help you bag them up."

"Wonderful. We'll start in Ben's closet." She tapped Ben's arm, and when he tried to protest, she placed a finger over his mouth. Madelyn turned back to Eric. "So, this drive is happening at Bridge of Music?"

"No, actually, it's at the local dance studio, run by a single mom of one of my kids." He turned to put his half-full bowl in the sink.

"And there it is!" She presented her hands, as if she had found the missing evidence.

"There what is, exactly?" Ben was confused by her supposed deposition.

"Mr. Sunshine over there." Madelyn waved her hands in Eric's direction. "It's because he's interested in the mom. He didn't finish eating, his back is to us..." She trailed off.

"No matter where he goes, Eric has consistently had the good fortune of a woman on his arm. But I credit you, big bro, for always staying true to yourself and not settling for anyone who isn't right for you. She's out there, Eric. You'll find her." Ben kissed Madelyn's cheek and draped an arm over her shoulders. "I'm grateful I found my one and only. Always has been, always will be you, Madelyn."

She snuggled into his side and wrapped an arm around his waist. "And you're the only man for me...but we're still going through your closet first."

Eric turned to face them, placing his elbows on the counter as he leaned his back against it. "It's different this time. She's...too many words come to mind, but none of them do her justice. And her kid, he's captivated me too."

Madelyn and Ben exchanged a knowing glance. "We're thrilled for you, Eric, and we very much look forward to meeting them! I want to hear more, but later. I have to go to the bathroom again."

As Madelyn waddled out of the kitchen, Ben strode over to Eric and gave his brother a bear hug. "Does this mean you might stick around here for a while?"

"I just might."

"What about Copenhagen?"

"I haven't heard yet. I put in for the professorship at the university at the same time I applied for Bridge of Music. I was told then that it could be some time before a decision is made, since the position isn't available until late February."

"Okay, well, I think you should focus on what you have here and figure out how you really feel about everything, what your heart wants for the long term. I mean, besides having the best brother in the world!" Ben spread his arms and smiled confidently.

"Thanks, little bro," Eric chuckled.

"You do remember, though, that we have to kick you out of the guest room soon? Madelyn's mom will be arriving the week before the baby is due, and staying for a couple of weeks. Then, once she leaves, mom and dad will be flying in from North Carolina to stay here for a while. We only have the one guest room. Of course, you're welcome to stay on the couch in the basement, but I would be happy to look at apartments with you, if you want."

"Yeah, I remember. Thanks so much for helping me out, Ben. I know you've got a lot going on to get ready for the baby, and I'm looking forward to meeting my nephew. I'll probably stay in the basement."

"You've helped me out plenty of times, too. You know, if you stay, Madelyn will have you on diaper rotation…"

Eric laughed heartily and again patted his brother on the back.

* * *

Leah and JJ enjoyed a walk on Main Street. The temperature was finally above freezing and coupled with the cloudless sunny sky, felt almost balmy; such was the nature of New England weather. The snow was just about gone, replaced by slushy puddles on the cement and muddy pockets on lawns. JJ was splashing his way down the sidewalk, reminiscent of Gene Kelly's classic scene in *Singin' In The Rain.*

As soon as Leah opened the door to Kay's Canines, barks and howls greeted her and JJ. The front desk was unmanned, but both Kay and Stef were behind the glass window that looked into the entryway. Each was at a different grooming table with a different dog, and they both waved enthusiastically at Leah and JJ.

JJ ran up to the window and pressed his hands against the glass. "Hi Aunt Kay! Hi Stef! Hi puppies!" He jumped up and down, expressing a few gleeful noises.

"Where is my undercoat rake?" Stef held up her hands and paced around her table, while a husky tried to follow her.

"How should I know where your undercoat rake is?" Kay responded, while her attention remained focused on the little Yorkie's teeth that she was in the process of cleaning.

"Well, I can't find my undercoat rake, and poor Skai here is waiting on me. I need my undercoat rake!" Stef bent down to fiddle through the supplies on the rack, while Skai let out a series of whimpers.

"Okay, fine, you can use my undercoat rake." While she kept her eyes and one hand on the Yorkie, Kay expertly passed the undercoat rake to Stef.

Kay and Stef are definitely two of a kind, Leah thought fondly. They met while in the same course for their dog grooming certifications and quickly became inseparable. Kay finished with the Yorkie, who was gently placed in a kennel, then she went around the corner to greet Leah and JJ.

"Hugs!" JJ opened his arms.

Kay returned the affection. "Do you want to pet the puppies?"

"Yes, it's amazing!"

"Okay, let's go, but remember…"

"I already know. 'Be gentle and don't touch anything else.'" JJ did his best impression of Kay.

Kay laughed and turned to Leah as they walked into the kennel area. "How are things?"

"We're good, just out for a walk. He swam a whole lap and back the other day!" Leah replied. "Are you sure that you and Stef can watch him during the donation drive?"

"That's great, and absolutely!" Kay took out the Yorkie, who licked JJ's hand.

Leah noticed that most of the kennels were occupied. "Busy today, huh?"

"Yeah, we've got some new dogs, which is great, but exhausting. Two of the dogs we've been training will be entering in state dog shows."

"Wow, that's really exciting! You'll have to let me know how they place."

"I'm going to play with Mr. Eric tomorrow!" JJ piped in.

"What now?" Kay questioned.

"Well, JJ, remember, he's coming over so you can do more singing with him," Leah clarified.

"Yes, and then he can play with me."

"Maybe. We'll see. But first, singing."

"Looks like JJ is bonding well with his new teacher." Kay put the Yorkie back in his kennel.

Leah handed JJ the mini-iPad from her bag, and he sat down to play games. "Yeah, Eric is working with JJ on singing. I'm hopeful this will be good for him."

"And good for you too?"

"I'll admit, he is a very charming, well-educated man, with a passion for his work and the kids."

"I suspect there's more to it than that." Stef joined them, after a high-five with JJ.

"Okay, yes…there is," Leah admitted. "But Eric's traveled to cities across the country and throughout Europe. So, what happens when he's ready for his next adventure, and leaves? I can't go through that again, and I can't put JJ through that, either. Whatever I'm feeling, I can control it." She spoke quietly so JJ wouldn't hear, grateful he was focused on his games.

Kay and Stef wrapped their arms around each other, then brought Leah into their embrace. Kay offered her wisdom and comfort. "We hear you, Leah," she said, "but some feelings are what they are and can't be controlled. And what if he stays? Taking a risk can be terrifying, we totally understand, but if the risk turns into something positive and real, your life could be even more fulfilling than it already is now and so could JJ's. You'll never know how good it could be, if you don't take the first step and explore what you're feeling. Whatever happens, Leah, you and JJ will always have us."

"Um, yeah, what she said," Stef concurred.

"Love you both." Leah pulled them in a little closer.

"I want hugs too!" JJ wiggled himself into the middle of the huddle.

* * *

Leah tried to convince herself that she had a very good reason to call Eric. She nodded her head, then tapped "call."

"Well, hello, Leah."

"Hi, Eric. Sorry to bother you, but I wanted to talk to you about JJ."

"No bother, it's very nice to hear your voice. Is JJ okay?"

"Yeah, he's fine. He's playing Mario Kart, so I only have a few minutes, because he might interrupt me."

"Okay, what's up?"

"He has it in his head that you'll be playing with him tomorrow. I think he's associating your coming here as more of a playtime rather than a singing lesson. I keep telling him that the lesson will be first. I'm extremely embarrassed to ask this, but would you have the time to play with him for a little while after the lesson? Only if you don't mind, of course, though I completely understand if it's not feasible."

"Play is a useful therapeutic tool, one I frequently use to aid in accomplishing a set goal," Eric said. "I'd be pleased to spend some playtime with JJ after our lesson."

"Thank you." Leah was relieved. She knew JJ would be very happy, and admittedly, she felt brightened as well. Eric intrigued her, and she was looking forward to the additional time with him. "JJ will likely want to go to the playground, so I recommend bringing boots, because it might be muddy. Also, I know we scheduled Monday for you to come here, but I think it would be best to transition him to Bridge of Music, instead. I think he'll be able to focus on singing more effectively if he's not continuing to expect playtime. This would require a plan to prepare him for this, tomorrow. What do you think?"

"I understand. I agree with you that JJ needs to focus on our goal," he replied. "I can always incorporate play as an earned reward at the end of our lesson at Bridge of Music. Tomorrow, I'll tell him that, at the beginning of each lesson, we'll set a goal and that our first goal will be to agree to have lessons at Bridge of Music starting

Monday. In addition, I'll assure JJ that I'll meet him at the door to walk him in the building and into the lesson room and will remind him that no one but me will hear him sing. I can also offer for you to stay in the room, if he wants you there, which should ease his anxiety. Are you comfortable with this plan?"

Leah was more than comfortable with his plan. She was extremely impressed by Eric's thoroughness and relieved to hear how well he understood JJ's needs. Her own anxiety slipped away. "This sounds wonderful, Eric. I can't thank you enough."

"You're very welcome, and it's you I have to thank."

"For what?"

"Talking with you has made my day."

"Oh…"

Eric chuckled, picturing the endearingly shy expression on Leah's face he was becoming fond of. "Until tomorrow. Goodnight, Leah."

"Goodnight, Eric," she whispered softly, then ended the call and exhaled.

Chapter Five

"He's here! Mr. Eric is here, Mommy!" JJ shouted with excitement. He'd been staring out the window in anticipation of Eric's arrival.

"Okay, let's go downstairs and let him in." Leah had just finished straightening up in the living room.

Just as the doorbell chimed, JJ threw open the door. "Hi!" he said, enthusiastically jumping up and down.

"Well, what a nice greeting! I'm very happy to see you, too, JJ. Are you ready for our lesson?" Eric stepped inside, then glanced over at Leah with a smile.

"Yes! It's amazing!"

"Great! Please calmly walk up the stairs, and decide where you want us to sit. I'd like to say hello to your mom, then I'll be up. Okay?"

"Okay!" JJ was off, not entirely calmly, but at least he didn't run.

"Thanks for coming, Eric," Leah said. "He's been watching out the window for you!"

Leah's hair was down, smooth and straight, and the length caressed her shoulders. She was dressed in brown woolen leggings and a green chenille sweater that draped over her hips and past her wrists, the color of the sweater highlighting the golden specks in her eyes. She looked warm and inviting. Eric widened his stance.

"Glad he's excited this time. No Dance World sweatshirt today?" he asked lightly.

With a gentle laugh, she replied, "Not today, though there *are* times that I wear my dance clothes on my days off."

"You look lovely, Leah." His voice went deep, mellow.

She lowered her lashes and smiled softly over her shoulder, opening the door to the apartment. "Thank you," she whispered.

"I'm ready!" JJ bounced on the couch. "You can sit here this time, Mr. Eric." He tapped the couch by his side. "You can go in the kitchen, Mommy."

"Okay, have fun!" Leah said, then did, in fact, go into the kitchen to clean up from lunch.

Eric placed his guitar on the floor, then faced JJ, picked up the boy's hands, one on top of the other, and placed his own hands around them. "Breathing is very important for singing, JJ," he explained. "I want you to take three deep belly-breaths with me."

Leah was amazed by how quickly Eric was able to calm JJ and gain his attention. She heard Eric as he talked to JJ about the transition plan to Bridge of Music and couldn't believe it when JJ complied without a protest. She *wished* she had that kind of superpower! Then, music and song began to fill her home.

After a few vocal warm-ups, Eric circled back to "You've Got a Friend In Me," since JJ had claimed that he knew all the words. "Okay, JJ, I'm going to start singing, but when I stop, you'll sing the missing word. Try to stay in rhythm with the guitar. Got it?"

JJ stood next to Eric and nodded. Then, Eric began with the song's intro, playing fingerstyle on the guitar and singing the first line, except for the last word.

JJ spoke that word, rather than sing.

Eric nodded his head, continuing to sing. A delighted expression spread across his face when he heard JJ progress to singing lightly. Catching JJ's eyes, Eric winked at the boy, infused with affection for their budding friendship, comparable to the song they were singing.

With a smile in his eyes and a bounce on his heels, JJ caroled, gaining confidence with each word.

Impressed by JJ's knowledge of the lyrics and his musical timing, Eric said, "Great job! Make sure to take a deep breath in each time before you sing. Let's try it again."

About a half hour later, the sound of running feet rolled from room to room, until JJ found Leah in the laundry room. "Mommy! I did it, Mommy!"

She put the basket down and hugged him. "That's great! Did you have fun?"

"Yes!"

Eric caught up to them. "He did really well. He started with one word to finish my line, then he sang phrases. He's got a great ear to keep himself in rhythm."

"That's amazing, JJ! I'm so proud of you."

"Yay! Can we go play outside now?"

Bundled in coats and boots with a ball in tow, the three of them headed toward the playground. Leah grabbed JJ's hand before they crossed the street. JJ slipped his other hand into Eric's, and looked up at him with a wide Duchenne smile. As Eric returned the expression, he felt a sense of connectedness, of belonging.

The playground was filled with swings, monkey bars, a rock-climbing wall, and a slide. On that day, only two families utilized the play structures. JJ stopped at the adjoining baseball field, since it was empty.

"Let's play tag. You're it!" JJ tagged Eric, then ran in the opposite direction.

"Oh, that was sneaky, JJ!" Eric was already on the chase. "Let's see how fast you can run!"

JJ laughed as he dodged Eric's reach, then changed direction. Eric pretended to be out of breath, then sped back up. Leah was entertained by the scene on the field and took a short video of it on her phone. Her heart was warmed as she watched JJ, so carefree, and heard his laughter. Her admiration for Eric grew as she observed his spirited, yet gentle, interaction with her son.

Then, Eric caught up with JJ, wrapped his arms around JJ's waist, and spun him around. "Gotcha! You're it!"

JJ squealed with delight. When Eric put him down, he was a little dizzy and dropped to the ground, though he continued to laugh. Eric took the opportunity and swiftly moved out of range, but JJ quickly recovered and went after him. Then, he saw Leah and changed his course. "You have to run, Mommy!"

"Oh no!" Leah laughed, and tried to zig-zag her way around JJ. He was closing in on her, so she made a sudden turn to throw him off. Unwittingly, she ran hard into Eric's arms. "Ooh!" she gasped.

His fleece hoodie was unzipped, and her arms pressed against the navy blue sweater that hugged his chest. He smelled of cedar and citrus, which enticed her senses. Leah's gaze landed on his full lips, temptingly surrounded by his black and white beard, then lifted to his eyes, where desire circled and radiated to her.

"You're it, Mommy!" JJ flew by and tagged her back.

Eric pulled Leah closer to him, her breath heavy, that appetizing mouth ajar. Long strands of hair had fallen pleasingly around her face, and her cheeks were flushed. At first, her eyes were wide with surprise, then quickly softened and sparkled. His hands wandered up her spine, then down again.

"You're it, Leah," he murmured, throaty and laden with double-meaning.

A shiver passed through her, though she wasn't cold. Leah opened her fists, palms circling Eric's chest, and felt the quickened pace of his heartbeat, just like her own. Her hands floated toward the back of his neck as she rose up onto her toes, closer to his lips. Suddenly, the corners of his mouth twisted up into a playful grin. Then, he ran, leaving her to stumble forward.

Leah caught her balance, then brought her fingers to her lips, feeling the yearning still lingering there. She wasn't quite sure what had just happened; it had only been a matter of seconds, yet had felt like an eternity. She blinked to clear her head, then heard JJ's laughter.

JJ was next to Eric, and the pair made silly faces at her. She scrunched her nose and smirked back at them, then ran toward them. They were both too fast for her, but she eventually caught up to JJ.

"Ha, you're it!" Leah quickly tagged him, then leaped away. Shortly after, she called over, "JJ, I'm out now. I need to sit down for a bit." She walked over to the bleachers.

JJ ran over to the ball they brought. "Mr. Eric, can you play catch with me?"

"Sure!"

Leah was able to get a few good pictures of them before JJ declared he was ready to go home.

"Okay," she said, "I just want one happy selfie, then we can go." Leah walked over to JJ and put an arm around him.

"Oh, Mommy," JJ sighed.

"I'll take it for you," Eric offered as he pulled out his phone. "Say 'cheese!'"

"No, Mr. Eric, you need to be in the selfie too!"

Eric looked to Leah for approval. She smiled and waved for him to join. JJ stood in the middle, while Leah draped an arm over his shoulder and leaned close to his head. Eric bent down close to JJ and tilted his phone up until all three faces were clearly in the frame.

"Say 'selfie!'" JJ sang with a wide smile, and Eric captured the happy moment.

"Who wants hot chocolate?" Leah cheerfully asked, grabbing the ball.

"Me!" JJ exclaimed, taking it from her. "Mr. Eric, do you want hot chocolate too?"

"That sounds…amazing!" Eric tickled JJ's sides.

"Yay!" JJ giggled.

As they walked back home, Leah asked Eric, "Are you sure you have the time to come back inside? We aren't keeping you from anything, are we?"

"I have no other commitments today, and it would please me to go back inside. JJ's very hard to say no to, as are you." Eric smiled warmly at her.

"It would make me happy too." Leah linked her hand in his, and smiled softly.

Back in the kitchen, she took down three mugs. "Eric, would you prefer coffee?"

"No way! Hot chocolate, please. Right, JJ?" Eric animated his reply.

"With marshmallows!"

"Coming up." Leah poured enough milk in the pot for three and set the stove to warm, then added cocoa to the mugs.

"Can I go play *Mario Kart*, Mommy?" JJ asked.

"That's fine. I'll let you know when the hot chocolate is ready."

"Mr. Eric, can you play with me?"

"It's been a very long time since I've played video games. You'll have to show me how first, okay?"

"Okay." JJ grabbed Eric's hand.

As Eric was pulled away, Leah cupped her hands around her mouth and wished him, "Good luck!" His exaggerated, worried expression made her laugh.

The afternoon flew by, Leah's home filled with a lot of laughter. The day was airy and light. *That was something*, she realized, *that JJ and I had really needed.* Leah was genuinely saddened that the day was coming to an end.

"JJ," she said, "it's a school night, so we'll have to soon say bye-bye to Mr. Eric."

"Aww," JJ whined. "Can he stay for dinner?"

"I'm going to order from the Pizzeria, if you would like to join us," she offered.

"Thanks, that would be nice. JJ, I plan to say goodbye after dinner so that I don't interrupt your school night routine, deal?"

"Deal!"

Once dinner had been delivered, they gathered at the table. Leah, once again, put a piece of carrot, along with a cucumber slice, on JJ's plate, which he proceeded to remove.

Eric made a show of taking a bite into his pizza, then having a forkful of salad. "Mmm! JJ, do you know what makes pizza taste even better?"

"What?"

"The salad!"

"Eww!" JJ watched, however, as Eric put a cucumber slice on his fork and into his mouth without hesitation. JJ slowly picked up the cucumber slice on his placemat, gave it a sniff, then, ever-so-delicately, touched his tongue to it. He scrunched his face and put it back on his placemat.

"Good job trying, buddy," Eric laughed.

Leah laughed, too, at JJ's response. Inside, she became even more amazed at Eric's way with JJ. "I'm not much of a cook, especially with this picky one here," she said, giving JJ a quick hug, "but I make as many healthy choices as I can for both of us, with treats mixed in, of course."

"I can see that. You're wonderful, Leah." Eric reached across the table and covered her hand with his, giving it a reassuring, comforting squeeze.

After dinner was cleaned up, Leah and JJ walked Eric downstairs. With his guitar over his shoulder, Eric kneeled down and looked into JJ's eyes, as he held the boy's hands. "You had a great lesson today, buddy, and I had so much fun with you. Thank you for today. Do you remember our plan for tomorrow?"

"I remember. Hugs!" JJ threw his arms around Eric's neck.

Eric closed his eyes and slowly wrapped his arms around JJ. The tender embrace touched his heart. When he stood up and looked at Leah, he saw her tears of joy and brushed a droplet off her cheek with his thumb. "See you tomorrow."

She was too emotional to speak; all she could do was nod her head. Then, he slipped out the door.

"Are you crying, Mommy?" JJ asked.

"Happy tears, sweet face."

Somehow, Leah found the strength to compose herself and get JJ into bed. "Tomorrow, it'll be exciting to have your singing lesson at Bridge of Music!" she said.

"Yeah, but I'm a little nervous too."

"Mr. Eric will meet us at the door, and I can go in with you, if you want."

"I know," JJ said. "Were you hugging him at the playground?"

"Well, yes. I guess I was."

"Do you like him, Mommy?"

"I do like him. Very much."

"I do, too. Can he come over again?"

"I hope so," she replied. "You need to go to sleep now, though. I love you!"

"I love you, Mommy." They snuggled for a bit, then Leah quietly left his room.

* * *

Later that evening, as Leah was about to go to bed, a text came through on her phone. Eric had sent her the selfie of the three of them, captioned: *I look forward to finishing what we started at the playground…*

Leah closed her eyes and felt it all over again.

Same, she texted in return.

Chapter Six

Leah had just picked JJ up from school, and they were on their way to Bridge of Music. He was unusually quiet.

"How was math today?" she asked, trying to get him to talk about his favorite class.

"I don't want to tell you right now."

Her son loved math, and under typical circumstances, he was always excited to talk about math class. The fact that he didn't want to showed Leah that JJ was nervous about his singing lesson at Bridge of Music. That novelty was at the front of his mind. She knew that math class had likely gone fine, as it always did, and she also knew that if she probed further regarding math, or anything else, for that matter, it would only increase JJ's anxiety about the singing lesson. So, they finished the drive in silence.

Eric was outside when he saw Leah pull into the parking lot. As they rounded the corner, he noticed that JJ was walking with his head down.

"Look, JJ, Mr. Eric is at the door," Leah reassured him, but he didn't look up. Then, with a concerned look on her face, she shook her head at Eric.

"I'm so glad to see you, JJ." Eric bent his knees in an effort to make eye contact with the boy. "Ms. Nicole and Ms. Lydia are inside. You can say hi if you want to, but it's also fine if you don't. There are only two parents in the waiting area, and two students are in music rooms upstairs, so it's quiet and not too busy. Do you want your mom to come with us?"

JJ nodded his head.

"That's fine, she can come in. Do you want to hold my hand?"

JJ hugged Eric's arm tightly to him.

Eric smiled and smoothed JJ's hair with his free hand. "Okay, this works too." He opened the door and brought JJ inside. He had already spoken to Lydia and Nicole, so they were anticipating JJ's arrival.

Leah waved as she passed Lydia, who gave a thumbs up, and Nicole, who pumped her fists in the air.

Eric walked straight through the waiting area and up the stairs. As they passed by the two occupied lesson rooms, Eric pointed out that the hallway was quiet. "Can you hear anything, JJ?"

JJ shook his head.

"There are students in these two rooms, but we can't hear them. It'll be the same thing in my room. You can sing as loud as you want, and no one will hear you, except your mom and me."

He opened the door to his room. Once they were inside and the door had been closed, JJ released his grip on Eric's arm. "Can you play your guitar now?"

"Yes, buddy. You're doing great so far."

"No, I'm doing amazing!"

"Yes, you're doing amazing!" Eric began to strum his guitar.

Standing by the door in the small room, Leah wiped her tears away. *Even if JJ doesn't sing,* she thought, *he had achieved a successful transition.*

Eric performed "Brave" by Sara Bareilles and JJ turned to Leah, jumping excitedly. As soon as Eric finished, JJ exclaimed, "Special Olympics, Mommy!"

"Good memory, JJ!" Leah said, then informed Eric, "The USA Special Olympics games were televised this past summer. JJ and I watched what we could of them, and found the athletes very inspirational. Sara Bareilles was there, and she performed 'Brave' live. It was the theme song for the games."

"Thank you for telling me that," Eric replied, "but I played it for you, though, JJ. I hope you know how brave it was that you came here today. Are you ready to sing with me?"

"Yes! You can go to the waiting area now, Mommy."

"I love you!" She quickly hugged JJ and left the room.

As soon as Leah was in the waiting area, Nicole ran over to her and threw her arms around her shoulders. "Wow, he did so well!"

"Yeah, that was incredible," Leah said. "And Eric has such a wonderful way with JJ."

"Looks like a lot has happened this past week!"

"Yes, that's true."

"I want to hear all about it," said Nicole. "You know, he talks about you and JJ to Lydia and me on a personal level, not the professional way he speaks about other families."

"Really?"

"Really! Now, *you* talk!" Nicole grabbed Leah's hand and walked her behind the desk. The pair chatted and caught up with each other's lives, and before they knew it, JJ and Eric had returned.

"Yay!" JJ exclaimed, hugging Leah.

"How did it go?"

"Amazing!"

"I'm so proud of you! Can you say hi to Ms. Nicole?"

"Hi!" While bouncing on his toes, he swung his arms over his head.

"Hi, JJ! I'm so glad you're having fun learning to sing." Nicole replied.

Leah went around to the front of the desk, where Eric leaned against it. "Did it really go well?" she asked, voice and eyes filled with hope.

"It really went well. He made good progress on his breathing and projecting a quality tone."

"You're amazing, Eric," Leah said. "The way you are with JJ, your music, your voice…you've brought music into our lives, and it means a lot to me. *You* mean a lot to me and to JJ." She touched his arm with one hand, the other resting upon her heart.

Her words and touch sparked Eric's heart. "Thank you. Both of you mean a lot to me as well." He took Leah's hand in his, stroking her palm.

Alluring sensations darted through Leah, but before she could think about it, JJ bounded over.

"Thank you, Mr. Eric! See you tomorrow at music class!" He hugged Eric's waist.

"Yes you will, buddy." Eric one-arm hugged JJ and patted his back. "Leah, I did want to talk to you about scheduling another lesson, and I have a question as well. Do you have a few minutes?"

"Actually, I don't, I'm sorry. I have to get back to the studio for a class."

"I'll call you tonight, then?"

"I'll look forward to it." She waved to Eric and Nicole, as JJ pulled her out the door.

* * *

Leah was snuggled with JJ for bedtime. He was tucked under the blankets up to his chin, while she was on top of the blankets on her side, one arm propping her head up. The bedroom was shadowed with the light from the hallway.

"Will I have another singing lesson with Mr. Eric?" JJ asked.

"Definitely yes, but I just don't know when yet."

"At Bridge of Music?"

"Yes."

JJ rolled onto his back and looked up at the ceiling in contemplation. "I like singing, and I know where Mr. Eric's room is now. I can do it, Mommy."

"I know you can, and I'm glad that you know so too." She leaned over for a hug. "Night night, sweet face."

"I love you, Mommy."

"Love you too."

* * *

After JJ's school lunch and backpack were prepped, the kitchen cleaned, and her face scrubbed, Leah crawled under her own blankets to read before sleep. Her phone rang, and she was delighted to see that it was Eric calling in.

"Hi Eric!"

"Hi, Leah. Sorry for calling this late. An issue came up with a student that required my intervention. I hope I didn't wake you."

"I understand. I was just getting into bed, but wasn't asleep. I'm glad you called."

Eric's thoughts momentarily wandered to the image of her. "Um...so, I'm wondering if JJ could come in for another lesson on Friday, same time?"

"Sure, we can make that work. He told me that he's fine now, so you won't have to meet us outside. I'm still in awe of how well you can get through to him."

"I'm glad to hear it, and thank you. He's a really great kid," Eric said. "Leah, I'd also like to talk to you about the winter concert."

"Okay, what do you want to know?"

"Lydia told me that it's a town-sponsored fundraiser for local food pantries, and I know about the different performances and vendors who participate. This is such a wonderful event, and I'm honored that two out of the ten participating students from Bridge of Music are my kids. I heard that your dance team performs, as well."

"Yes, that's all true," she replied. "Lydia makes sure accommodations are made for all her students, and it's a wonderful way to spread awareness too. It's so great that two of the students are yours. You'll really enjoy the concert! And yes, the dance you saw my team rehearsing is the one for the concert."

"Ah, your dancers will bring down the house, for sure. Does JJ attend?"

"Thanks! He does go. He enjoys the music, and I want him to support the kids from Bridge of Music. My sister stays with him because I'm busy with my team and mingling with guests. JJ usually lets my sister know when he's ready to go home, as the crowd can get to be too much for him."

"I'm thinking of signing him up as a performer," Eric said, "and would like your input."

She hadn't been expecting that; her mind raced with all sorts of worry.

"Leah?"

"I don't know, Eric. JJ's never performed by himself before. He's only done school shows for his grade, with his class. The winter concert is a large event. It's only two and a half weeks away, and—"

"Okay, Leah." Eric interrupted her. "It wasn't my intention to cause you unease. I'm sorry. Can we please change to video, so I can see your face?"

"Okay."

Eric flipped the call to video mode. Leah's beautiful face was filled with angst, which he had caused. "I'm truly sorry that I've upset you. Please hear me out."

"Okay."

"I'm thinking that I could perform with him, similar to what we do in our lesson. JJ can stand next to me, and it'll be more of a 'show what you know' rather than a rehearsed performance. He's comfortable with 'You've Got a Friend In Me,' so we'll stick with that, and I'll prepare him and structure as much as I possibly can. I'll call the high school to see if there's a time I can bring him there to get on the stage before the concert," Eric explained. "I'll be there with him every step of the way. He won't be alone. Even if all he does is stand next to me, I think this will be good for him and good for the town. Honestly, Leah, I think he can do this. Of course, I'll talk to him, and if, at any point, JJ decides that he doesn't want to do this, we won't. I won't go against your wishes, though."

"Are you performing with your other students?"

"No, but they requested to perform and already understand the process. That's not the case for JJ."

"Why do you want him to do this?"

"He's already made such big leaps in a very short amount of time, and I think this will be very positive for his confidence and self-esteem. JJ shines in my eyes, and I want him to see that in himself."

At that, Leah turned away with her eyes tightly shut, bringing a closed hand to her lips. Her eyes were misty, as she opened them to look at him. "You're very persuasive, Eric Hynes."

"When there's something I want, I go after it, Leah Preston." His innuendo permeated through the screen.

Leah finally released her worry with a deep breath. Her expression lightened, and she blinked the tears away. *He always seemed to know how to ignite my emotions*, she thought. With a tilt to her head, she smiled with a slight sideways curve to her lips, lashes fluttering. Her hair fanned over her cheek.

"And there's the look that gets me every time…" Eric wished he could reach through the phone to brush her hair off her face. "Are you okay now?"

"I think so. Last question, does Lydia know about this?"

"Yes. She thinks it's a great idea."

With a nod, Leah agreed. "Okay. Sometimes, though, even when JJ seems excited about something, he can freeze up and refuse to move in the moment. It's very hard to get him through that, especially now that he's bigger and I can't just pick him up. A few times, I've been able to bring him out of it and move forward, but other times we've had to turn around and go home."

"I hear you. I've helped families through crises before. If it happens, we'll deal with it then. Like I said, he won't have to do this if he doesn't want to. I just want to help him try." Eric paused. "One final thought. Because JJ likely associates the concert with you, I think I should be the one to introduce this idea to him first. I'll let you know how it goes, and then you can talk to him. Okay?"

"Okay, let's try."

"You're very strong for taking this step, Leah. I hope you know that."

"I often don't feel strong, though."

"I can understand that," he said softly. "I'm here for you. You don't need to go through these things alone. Not anymore."

"That means more than I can say."

"Have a good sleep, Leah."

"You, too. Goodnight, Eric."

Chapter Seven

"Yes, Mrs. Jones, this Sunday afternoon…Certainly, we will definitely provide diapers…You're very welcome. See you then!"

Leah hung up with the director of one of the family shelters she worked with for her donation drive. She'd reached out to most of the shelters, but wasn't yet finished. She also needed confirmations from her dancers' parents as to how many could help with the deliveries. Because she was focused on the lists in front of her, she didn't look at the caller ID when her phone chimed.

"Good morning, Dance World! How may I help you?"

"Technically, it's afternoon, and I believe I called your personal cell. But yes, you may help me," the genial voice replied.

Leah looked at the clock on the wall, then the phone in her hand. *Goodness,* she thought, *where had the morning gone?* "Oh hi, Eric. Sorry about that. I've been busy with donation preparations, and I guess I lost track of the time. How are you?"

"I'm cold, actually. Would you kindly help me by coming to your front door?"

"What? Why?" she asked, walking over to the front door. "What are you doing here?" Leah spoke into the phone, though she looked at him through the glass with a confused expression on her face.

Eric laughed, then hugged his arms in a show of how cold it was outside.

"Oh, of course…" Leah realized the phone was still by her ear, so she disconnected the call and unlocked the door.

"Hi there." He relaxed into the warmth of the indoors. "Have you had lunch yet?"

"Actually, I haven't eaten anything yet today."

"Well, it's a good thing I brought you lunch, then." He handed her the bag he held.

"That's so sweet of you, though it wasn't…" Leah was delightfully surprised when she saw the contents of the bag. "I *love* Jenny's chicken noodle soup and homemade bread! How did you know? Thank you so much!"

"You're very welcome. Make sure to eat it now, while it's still hot."

"Can you join me?"

"I want to say yes, but I can't. I have a parent meeting coming up."

"Okay. Well, let me just get my wallet—"

She turned away, but Eric reached for her arm. "You've given me the joy of seeing your smile light up your eyes. That's all I need." He gently stroked her cheek, then headed back out into the cold.

Skin still tingling from his touch, a thought came to her. Before he got too far away, Leah flung open the door and shouted, "Wait! What's your favorite meal?"

Eric turned, and while he walked backwards, he answered, "Irish lamb stew does it for me!" He waved as he turned back around toward his car.

Back at her desk, Leah moved her papers out of the way and opened the soup container. The scent of the chicken, fresh vegetables, noodles, and broth wafted around her, and she was reminded of childhood, of playing in the house while her mom was in the kitchen, stirring the large pot of soul restoring soup. Its comforting smell had permeated all three floors of her childhood home. She smiled in warm remembrance while she enjoyed every spoonful.

That really hit the spot, she thought. Then, she typed "Irish lamb stew recipes" into the search engine on her phone.

* * *

While JJ was in music class, Leah knocked on Lydia's office door.

"Leah, come on in."

"Hi, Lydia. If you have a minute, I'd like to ask you about JJ and the concert?"

"Sure, go ahead."

"Eric told me that you agree with his plan for JJ to sing in the concert," Leah said.

"Yes, don't worry," Lydia replied. "I'm not going to charge extra for any additional time Eric will need with JJ. You and I already discussed the flat fee increase for the weekly singing lesson, I'll leave it at that."

"Thank you, I appreciate that, but…do you think it's rushed to aim for a concert performance this year?"

"If JJ hadn't yet made progress, I'd say yes, but from what Eric's told me, JJ's progress has been unexpectedly swift. That's why I agreed to his plan. After the concert, yes, scale back to the weekly lessons, so JJ can focus on making further technical progress." Lydia rested her hands on Leah's shoulders. "Place trust in Eric, Leah. Open yourself and let him in. He has JJ's and your best interests at heart. I've seen it. I've seen how much he cares for both of you, intimately."

"Thanks, Lydia." Leah embraced the wise woman she was so fond of.

"Anytime, dear."

Once Leah was back in the waiting area, Nicole eagerly asked, "How was your lunch?"

"Ah, that's how he knew."

"I told him your favorite, but he came to me. It was all him."

"Mommy!" The door opened, and JJ bounded out of class. "It was amazing!"

"I'm so glad!"

As JJ tugged her toward the exit, she waved to Eric. "Thanks again for lunch! I really enjoyed it."

"My pleasure!" he replied.

* * *

Over the next couple of days, Leah was busy with final preparations for the donation drive, along with extra rehearsals for her dance team. She hadn't seen Eric, but he had texted her several times. Thoughts of him floated at the front of her mind, and she had a sunny energy as she went about her days.

Leah missed seeing him, though. Her heart warmed as her mind's eye brought into focus his incredibly handsome face, his solid body, his deep, raspy voice. The way she felt when he smiled at her, looked at her with that endlessly flowing sea of emotion in his eyes, the way he touched her...

She admired and respected Eric's strong sense of empathy and awareness, his intelligence and confidence, his gentle compassion and silly humor, his musicality. He understood JJ, and had connected with her son like no other.

Connected with *her* like no other.

The timer went off for the oven, and as Leah took the bread out, she smiled peacefully. This time, in her heart, it felt real. It felt *right*. A glimmer of hope sparked deep inside her. She closed her eyes and wished for the light to grow, everlasting.

It had been a very long time since Leah had cooked for someone other than JJ or herself. She actually enjoyed the process, and was proud of herself. She hoped it tasted as good as it smelled! Before she left for JJ's school pickup, she texted Eric.

Hi! I have a surprise for you. Can you come over for dinner tonight with JJ and me?

He was quick with a reply.

I'm very intrigued. I'll be there. Seven-fifteen okay? I won't be able to stay after dinner, though, as my parents decided to fly in tonight, earlier than they originally planned.

That's nice! I'll let JJ know. Seven-fifteen it is! See you in a bit for his lesson.

* * *

At Bridge of Music, JJ walked right in and up the stairs to Eric's room without hesitation. "Hi!" he said, skipping over to Eric.

"Hi, buddy, it's so nice to see you." Eric held up a hand for a high five with JJ.

"Mommy, you can go now."

"Have fun! Love you!" she said to JJ. Then, she offered Eric a delicate wave of her fingers. Before Leah left the room, she saw the ripples that rose in the ocean of his eyes, circling around his sea.

"Your mom is something else, buddy," Eric said, more to himself than to JJ, as he closed the door.

"Do you like her, Mr. Eric?"

"Ah…your mom? Yes, I like your mom a lot."

"Do you like me?"

Eric opened his arms and JJ leaned in. "JJ, I like you far beyond infinity!" he replied, spreading his arms wide then circling them around JJ again.

"Yay!" JJ laughed. "Me and Mommy like you a lot too, Mr. Eric."

Eric closed his eyes and held JJ a little tighter. Then, he released him, but held JJ's hands in his. "Our goal today is to make a plan for the winter concert. I signed us up to perform on the stage."

Eric felt the sudden tenseness in JJ, so he applied slight pressure to the boy's hands as a weighted, calming effect. "We'll just show what we know. You know 'You've Got a Friend In Me' very well. I'll bring a chair on the stage for me to sit and play my guitar, and you can stand next to me like you always do. We make a good team, and I think it would be really cool to do this with you. What do you think, JJ?"

"I can't sing in front of people."

"That's okay." Eric said lightly. "I'll sing, but I'll need your help. I can sing so much better when you're standing next to me, because you make me feel safe and strong. Will you help me?"

JJ thought about it for a minute, then released his tension. "Okay, I will help you."

Eric pulled JJ into another embrace. "That's amazing, buddy. Thank you."

"But I don't want them to turn the lights on. Sometimes, they turn the lights on for kids, but I don't want to see anyone. Except Mommy. I want to see Mommy."

"Deal! Would you want us to go first, last, or somewhere in the middle?"

"Last."

"And if the audience cheers for us, it's because they liked us."

"I usually block my ears for the cheering. Mommy always makes me wear an itchy shirt." JJ scrunched his nose.

Eric laughed. "I love that you block your ears when you need to. And yeah, I have to wear an itchy shirt too, and a tie, and a jacket."

"Eww!"

"But we'll look amazing!"

"I guess. Can you play your guitar now?"

"Yes, buddy."

Leah was chatting with Nicole when JJ came excitedly into the waiting area. "I'm going to help Mr. Eric at the winter concert, Mommy!"

"You are?" She was genuinely confused by that statement.

"Yes! He's going to sing on the stage, but he needs me to help him sing better."

"That's great, JJ! How are you going to help him?"

"I will stand next to him, because I make him strong."

"Wow, JJ, that's incredible!"

"No, it's amazing!"

"Very amazing!" Leah hugged JJ and looked up at Eric in astonishment.

* * *

"I can't see anything out the window, Mommy. It's too dark. When will Mr. Eric get here?"

"Any minute now." Leah finished JJ's mac and cheese, and put a lid on the pot to keep it warm.

The doorbell buzzed and JJ ran to the door. "Let's go, Mommy!"

Downstairs, JJ let Eric in. "Hi!"

"Hi, JJ. This is for you."

"Yay, vanilla cupcakes with white frosting! Look, Mommy!"

"For after dinner." She shook a finger at him. "Say 'thank you.'"

"Thank you!"

"You're welcome, buddy." Then, Eric turned his attention to Leah. "And this is for you." With the arm that had been behind his back, he presented her with a single white rose.

Leah looked into his adoring eyes, matching his gaze. *This January definitely marks a new year for new possibilities*, she thought, as she stepped closer to Eric and wrapped her arms around him. She angled the rose's delicate petals toward her so she could drink its fragrance. When he embraced her in return, she pulled him closer still. "Thank you. I've missed you, Eric."

"I've missed you too."

"Hugs!" JJ jumped up and down. "I want hugs!"

Leah and Eric laughed and brought JJ into their embrace.

Once upstairs, Eric hung up his coat and took a whiff of the scent that filled the apartment. "Mmm, that smells good. What is it?"

"Come sit down and I'll show you." Leah held his hand as they walked into the kitchen. She put the cupcakes in the refrigerator and filled a narrow vase with water for the rose, which became the decoration for the center of the table. She served JJ's mac and cheese first, then brought over two bowls of stew, placing one in front of Eric and the other on her placemat.

The astonished expression was now Eric's. "No, you did not! Is this…" He ate a spoonful. "This is Irish lamb stew!"

Then, she put the plate of sliced bread onto the table.

"*And* Irish soda bread?" He chose a slice and took a large bite.

"Surprise!" Leah smiled with glee at his reaction, then sat down.

"Oh, Leah, this is delicious! How did you…I thought you said you didn't cook?"

Leah ate her first spoonful, and was pleasantly surprised herself. "I said I'm not much of a cook, but I can look up and follow a recipe. The bread was actually quite simple, and I used the slow cooker for the stew. Do you really like it?"

"Are you kidding me? I feel like I'm in a Dublin pub right now. It's that good!" He tucked a few loose strands of Leah's hair behind her ear, and the endearing expression on her face went straight to his heart. "Thank you, Leah."

"You're very welcome. I'm so glad you like it!"

"What is a Dublin pub, Mr. Eric?" JJ asked.

Eric brought his attention to JJ and explained, "Dublin is the capital city in Ireland. I used to live there for a while. In Ireland, a pub is a bar that serves a variety of drinks, plus good food."

"Oh, okay. Boston is the capital of Massachusetts. Ireland is in Europe, next to the United Kingdom. I never lived there. I only live here."

"Excellent job knowing your geography, JJ!" Eric was highly impressed.

"I love maps," JJ replied, "and I find places on the computer. What are you and Mr. Eric eating, Mommy?"

"We are eating an Irish stew and bread, which are traditional foods in Ireland," she answered.

"And it's my favorite food to eat," Eric chimed in. "Your mom is very thoughtful to have made this for me."

"It's stinky." JJ covered his nose.

"Oh, buddy, I have to disagree with you on that one. You don't know what you're missing. It's really good." Eric savored another spoonful. "Mmm."

JJ picked up his spoon, stirring it into the small bowl Leah had provided for him with a sample of the stew. He scooped up two pieces. "Is this a potato and bacon, Mommy?"

"You're right!"

JJ sniffed the mixture on his spoon, then cautiously put it in his mouth. "It's okay, but I don't want any more. Can I try the bread, Mommy?"

"Absolutely! And I'm glad you tried the stew."

JJ took a bite of a slice of bread. "This is yummy," he decided. "I will finish this!"

"I'm so glad you like the bread, JJ! Eric, would you like another bowl?"

"Definitely! Yes, please."

Leah refilled Eric's bowl, then sat down to finish hers. One bowl would be enough for her; the stew was a very hearty meal.

"Can Mr. Eric play after dinner, Mommy?" JJ asked.

"JJ, we talked about this. Tonight, he can't stay, because his parents are visiting. We need to be grateful that he joined us for dinner."

"Why are your parents visiting, Mr. Eric?"

"Well, JJ, my brother, Ben, and his wife, Madelyn, are having a baby soon. My parents decided to fly back here before the baby arrives."

"Are they flying on an airplane? Where do they live?"

"Yes, they're flying on an airplane. They used to live not too far from here. That's where I lived when I was your age. Ben and Madelyn still live there, and I'm staying with them until I find my own place. My parents are older now and have retired from their jobs, so they decided to move to North Carolina."

"That's amazing! I want to do a trip across the United States. I have it all planned out."

"I'm sure you do. That's a great goal." Eric chuckled. "I think I'd like another selfie. JJ, come over between your mom and me."

"Oh, okay." JJ grudgingly walked over. Then, he smiled wide, as Leah and Eric scooted closer to him. "Say 'amazing!'"

Eric snapped the picture and immediately shared it to Leah's phone. He admitted to himself that he really wanted to capture another memory with Leah and JJ. He also admitted to himself that they were always on his mind.

JJ entertained Leah and Eric with the details of his visionary travel plan. Once they finished their meals, Leah and JJ walked Eric downstairs.

"I had fun with you, JJ." Eric ruffled his hair. He could tell that JJ was sad that the evening was cut short. He looked at Leah and brushed her cheek with the back of his hand. "This was incredible. Thank you, again."

"I'm so glad," she replied. "We enjoyed having you here. See you at the donation drive?"

"Definitely."

Eric's smile remained imprinted in her mind after he left, even after she and JJ went back upstairs.

Chapter Eight

Leah gave a pep talk to her dance team and their parents after they'd completed the setup for the donation drive.

"As always, I am beyond grateful to all of you for spending your Sunday afternoon helping me. This drive wouldn't be as successful as it is without all of you. There are two cases of water plus snacks in the office, so make sure to stay fueled up." She paused. "Well, I think we're ready to open the door. All hands in!"

They stood shoulder to shoulder in a circle. Everyone put their hands into the middle of the circle, then shimmied their hands up over their heads, chanting, "Dance World donation drive!" Cheers, claps, and high fives followed.

Everyone, including the parents, sported Dance World logo wear. As the sponsor of the drive, Leah felt it was important that her studio name be represented by all who assisted in the drive. She didn't mind if the style of clothing was different, so long as it had the Dance World logo on it. Leah preferred to wear the sweatshirt, while many were in t-shirts, and others had chosen tanks or fleece. She sold them all at her studio, and required that all students' logo wear be purchased. Any parent who assisted in the drive was given one logo wear item for free.

"Okay, places everyone!" Leah stood in the doorway of the studio. A folding table and chair were set up by the door, manned by one of the parents, Carolyn, and her daughter, Zelia. It was decorated not only with relevant information about the donation drive and the shelters that were being donated to but also with Dance World brochures and business cards, along with flyers for the winter concert. On both sides of Carolyn stood several of the students. Further into the studio was a row of large bins, generously donated to her by the owner of the local dry cleaner; in return, business cards for the dry cleaner had been added to the table. Several parents and students were stationed at each bin.

As people entered the building, they walked through the waiting area to be greeted by Carolyn, who asked what type of donations were being made. The students by the table were assigned to a specific item for donation, which corresponded to a specific bin. So, the appropriate student took the donation to their bin, tagged a student in their group to go to the table, then unloaded the donation into the bin with the help of their group. Finally, any bags or boxes used for donated items were then put into a recycling bin. Leah was fortunate to have enough volunteers for the flow of traffic to move quickly. This allowed her the ability to speak with everyone who came in, as well as to check on her team.

At exactly noon, Leah unlocked the door to the studio and the line that had formed outside began to file in. With a welcoming smile, she waved to everyone in line and walked into the studio with the first participant. "Lydia, you're always my line leader!"

"Yes, you know me, always eager to help support a good cause," she replied. "Hi, Carolyn. Women's clothes and shoes being donated today."

Leah glided past Lydia to stand behind the table, watching as her team went smoothly into action.

Within minutes, the studio was alive with efficient movement. Many of the donors remained inside the studio for a while, talking with Leah or various members of her team. Soon, the walls echoed with cheerful chatter.

Eric made his donation at the table, then stepped out of the way, along the inside wall of the studio behind the door. He watched Leah standing in the middle of the room, speaking to the few people beside her. Her gaze frequently shifted to the front table, and she waved at those who came in.

One of her students tapped her shoulder and whispered in her ear. She politely excused herself from the people she'd been speaking with and followed her student to a large bin at the other end of the studio. Leah assisted the group with switching out a few items from another large bin, motivating her team with a few words and a thumbs-up. As Leah turned around, an older woman opened her arms for a hug. The entire time, Leah had a warm smile on her face. She came back to the table, greeted the donor by name, then cheered on her team members. She seemed to know everyone who came in and was treated with high respect by both the patrons and her team. The atmosphere in the studio radiated with benevolence… all because of her.

Eric was in awe of her.

Then, Leah looked to her side and saw him. She patted the backs of the students she was standing next to, and crossed over to him. "I'm so glad you're here!"

"Leah, your grace and graciousness are inimitable," Eric said. "You inspire everyone around you."

She shyly lowered her head. "They've all helped me. I enjoy being able to give back."

He lifted her chin and looked in her eyes. "It shows. You're glowing. I am honored to be a witness. Go on back to your team. I don't want to keep you from them. I'm waiting for my family."

"It warms my heart that you're staying." Leah ran a hand gently along his forearm, then went back to her team.

As she approached the table, Debbie Irwin walked in with two bags. "Debbie, it's so good to see you!" Leah walked around the table and the two women hugged.

"You know I love you," she replied. "Where's my little guy? Oh, this bag is infant clothes, and this bag is infant blankets." Debbie handed the bags to Leah, who passed them to the students assigned to the corresponding bins.

Leah and Debbie walked into the studio, away from the traffic at the table. "I love you too. JJ's upstairs with my sister. He's not so little anymore. He's almost as tall as me!" Leah pulled out her phone and showed Debbie some recent pictures of JJ. As she scrolled through the pictures, the playground selfie came up.

"He's so adorable and starting to look so grown up! I miss JJ. Wait a minute, who's that?" Debbie pointed to Eric's face in the photo.

"Oh, that's right, you've been in California. We haven't seen you in a while. How's Brendan?"

Since Debbie and her husband had been retired, they frequently traveled to visit their grown children and grandchildren. "Well, he's a freelancer for TV and film production. We just got back yesterday, so I'm tired from jet lag," she said. "I've had those baby donations sitting in my closet since the last time we were in New York. Aaron's kids are in preschool and kindergarten now. No more babies. I just love them so much. We're going back to New York on Tuesday for a couple of days."

"They keep you very busy! I hope you'll be here for the winter concert. JJ will be on the stage for the first time."

"He will? With his music class?"

"No, with his speech therapist, who's teaching him to sing!" Debbie grabbed Leah's arm with a shocked expression on her face, and Leah pointed to Eric's face in the photo. "This is Eric, JJ's speech therapist."

"Well, I'll definitely be at the concert…but this picture looks very casual. Have you gotten cozy with this speech therapist?"

"We have been getting close," Leah admitted. "He's great with JJ, and he makes me feel things I never thought I would."

"It's about time." Debbie hugged Leah.

"Let me introduce you to him."

"He's here? Why didn't you say so? Show me."

Leah saw that Eric was in a conversation with the dad of one of his students. They shook hands, and the dad left as Leah and Debbie approached. "Eric, my good friend, Debbie Irwin, wants to meet you. Debbie, this is Eric Hynes, speech and language pathologist and music instructor at Bridge of Music."

"Pleasure to meet you, Mrs. Irwin." Eric flashed his winning smile and extended his hand.

"Debbie, please." She wrapped both her hands around Eric's, then looked at Leah. "He's so handsome."

Leah's gaze met Eric's and held. "Yes, very handsome. Inside and out."

Debbie gently squeezed her arm, which brought Leah back from drifting into Eric's eyes. "Eric, Debbie is the reason I'm able to do all of this." She spread her arms and looked around her bustling studio. "A decade ago, Debbie and her husband coordinated with a contractor friend of theirs to rebuild this entire building into the studio and apartment for JJ and me. And she's extremely generous with my rental fees."

Eric began to better understand Leah's desire to give back, but he wanted to know more. "That's quite extraordinary. You are a good friend indeed, Debbie."

She waved a hand. "I'd do anything for Leah and JJ. On that note, I will see you later, I need to go take a nap. Even with as many times as I've been to California, the jet lag is still exhausting." She hugged Leah one last time, squeezed Eric's arm, and left.

"Leah, what…" He stopped himself, realizing that it was not the time nor place to ask her questions.

"Oh, look!" Leah pointed to the table. "Nicole's here with the twins. Have you met her girls yet?"

"No, I haven't," Eric said and followed Leah to the table.

"Hi!" Nicole acknowledged them both. She had one daughter on either side of her, both with their noses in their phones. "Girls, say hi to Leah and Eric."

"Hi."

"Hey."

Both girls looked up only for the brief greeting, then went back to their phones.

"Nice to meet you both," Eric replied.

"Hopefully both of you can hang out with JJ soon," Leah added. Both girls looked at Eric, then each other, then nodded their heads at Leah.

"Teenagers." Nicole laughed. "I'm lucky that they're good kids! Okay, let's go, girls. Bye, Leah, bye, Eric!"

Leah and Eric laughed, waving as Nicole and her twins turned to leave. Then, Leah excused herself to check on her team members at the bins, and Eric saw that his family had arrived. Ben carried four bags, and his father carried several boxes of diapers. While they checked the donations in, Eric brought his mother, Madelyn, and her mother into the studio. "Good to see you again, Mrs. Dalton. Hi, Madelyn. Hi, mom." Eric kissed his mother on the cheek.

"Hello, sweetheart," Eric's mother said. "This is a lovely place. When can we meet Leah, the one you've been speaking so much about?"

"She's working on the donation bins with her students, but let me go ask her if she can talk to you now." He left his family in the middle of the room and found Leah behind one of the bins. She was collecting empty bags and putting them in the recycling bin as he approached. "Leah, my family is here. Do you have a few minutes to talk to them?"

"Oh, yes, of course." She threw the remaining bags in the bin, then sanitized her hands while she walked with Eric.

Eric noticed that Ben and his father had joined the women. "Leah, I'd like to introduce you to my parents, Patricia and Matthew

Hynes, my brother and his wife, Ben and Madelyn Hynes, and Madelyn's mom, Mrs. Heather Dalton." Then, he stepped behind Leah and rested his hands on her shoulders. "Everyone, this is Leah Preston, owner and director of Dance World. She's the organizer of this donation drive and an incredible woman I'm privileged to know." He gave her shoulders a light squeeze.

With her familiar shy smile, Leah looked over her shoulder at Eric in response to his commendatory introduction. Then, she focused forward on his family. "It's so nice to meet all of you! Thank you so much for coming." Leah moved to Eric's mother first and offered her hand in greeting.

Patricia took Leah's hand warmly. "What a lovely place you have here. On our way here, we purchased a few boxes of diapers to donate. We flew in from North Carolina, you see, though once we'd arrived, Eric told us about your wonderful donation drive and we wanted to help. Besides, we also wanted to stock up for our soon-to-arrive grandson."

"Thank you so much, Mrs. Hynes, for your kind words and thoughtful donation." Leah stepped back and opened her arms. "Congratulations to all of you on the baby-to-be!" She went over to Madelyn. "You poor thing, I can't believe you're still standing! Let me get you a chair."

Madelyn grabbed Leah's arm. "No, no. If I sit down, it'll take me an hour to get back up! Thank you, though. We brought four bags of donatable items."

Leah nodded her head. "I remember those days, too, when I had trouble sitting and standing! And thank you for your very generous donation." She stepped to Madelyn's side to shake Mrs. Dalton's hand, then to her other side to shake Ben's. Instead, Ben pulled Leah into an embrace.

"Oh!" She exclaimed.

"Hey, hey, watch your hands, little bro!" Eric humorously warned his brother.

"Ben!" Madelyn tapped his arm.

"What?" Ben feigned unawareness, releasing Leah. "Pleasure to finally meet you. My brother's told us a lot about you."

"All good things, I hope?"

"Definitely." Ben rested an arm around Madelyn's shoulders.

Leah then turned to Eric's father, who placed a hand above his heart and nodded his head with kind eyes and a gentle smile. *Apparently*, she thought, *all the Hynes men exuded charm!* Then, she greeted him similarly.

"Leah, dear, where is your son? We hoped to meet him as well." Patricia looked around the room, but didn't see any young children.

"Oh, he's upstairs in our apartment. My sister and her wife are with him. As you might have noticed, the studio echoes and gets loud with so many people. JJ gets very uncomfortable with that kind of volume. But…" She held up a finger, looking at the clock. "Very soon, I'll be locking the door to end the drop off period. My team will be here organizing the bins for deliveries, but it shouldn't be as loud, and if we step into the hallway, it should help to lessen the volume as well. Would you mind waiting for a bit? I certainly don't want to keep you from anything."

"We will be happy to wait," Patricia replied. "Now, we don't want to take up any more of your time, dear, while you're still busy."

"No worries. I'll be back!" Leah turned to Eric, holding his hand and his gaze for a moment. Then, she gracefully floated away, moving to greet the incoming patrons.

After a few minutes, Madelyn noticed there was a lull, so she went over to Leah. "Can I talk to you?"

"Sure! Would you like some water?"

"No, thanks, but you can show me where the bathroom is."

"Yes, the never-ending bathroom runs. I remember that, too!"

"I just wanted to say that Eric is a really good man with a big heart," Madelyn told her. "I've known him my entire life because, although he is ten years older than Ben and me, we grew up together as neighbors. Even though he travels a lot, we can always count on him when it truly matters. He's been very good to my mom, especially since we lost my dad, and he helped his parents move to North Carolina. He's seen Ben and me through a lot that life has thrown at us over the years."

"Madelyn, I'm so sorry to hear about your dad," Leah said. "I can sympathize. Both of my parents have passed. How are you and baby-to-be doing? Eric tells me that you're due any day now?"

"Thank you, and same to you. I'm sorry to hear about your parents," she replied. "We are very grateful that this pregnancy has been healthy. At this point, I just want him to come out already!"

"Thanks, and yes, I can relate to that feeling as well, even though JJ was two weeks early." Leah paused. "Madelyn, why did you tell me all that about Eric?"

"He's staying with us, and has been talking about you and JJ nonstop. I can also see the way the two of you look at each other. Eric has never behaved this way with any other woman. I just wanted you to know that."

Leah hugged Madelyn. "Thank you. I care for him very much."

"I can see that," Madelyn agreed.

A short time later, Leah walked the last patron to the door, then locked it. She turned the corner into the studio and announced, "Excellent job, everyone! Thank you all for your hard work! We did it!" She was met with a chorus of cheers. "Please, pack up the bins, and those of you who are driving for deliveries, come see me."

Several of the parents came forward. Leah confirmed that each parent had the correct name and address of the shelter they were delivering to, then handed them Dance World business cards to be given to the shelters' directors. She always followed up with phone calls to all the shelters' directors the day after every donation drive, so that she could be assured the deliveries were to their satisfaction. Then, she helped Carolyn and Zelia with the table and chair, though Eric and Ben quickly stepped in and took care of it.

Once her team was settled, Leah joined Eric and his family. "Thanks again for waiting. My team will be just a little while longer to get everything packed up into cars, but it's quieter now. I texted my sister to bring JJ down into the hallway, if all of you want to follow me?"

Leah opened the back door of the studio and waved to Kay and Stef, who waited in the hallway. JJ had his head down, and the bubble-popper fidget was in his hands. "Hi, sweet face!"

"Mommy!" He looked up at her, jumping up and down.

"Come give me a hug!" She opened her arms, and he ran into them. "JJ, Mr. Eric is here with his family. I would like you to say hi to them, and we can introduce them to our family."

"Can I say hi to Mr. Eric first?"

"Sure." Leah turned back into the studio and motioned for Eric and his family to come into the hallway. She kept an arm around JJ as they stepped back, allowing the others to enter.

JJ brought the popper fidget to his mouth and lowered his head, but lifted his eyes to see who came in. "Hi, Mr. Eric," he said softly.

Eric bent down in front of JJ. "Hi, buddy. I'm happy to see you. Did you have a fun afternoon?"

JJ nodded his head.

"Did you go to the playground?"

JJ shook his head.

"Did you climb a mountain?"

JJ shook his head, but he also lowered the popper away from his mouth and a small smile crept in.

"Did you sail on a boat?"

JJ laughingly shook his head. "No, Mr. Eric!"

"Oh. Hmm." Eric scrunched his brows and cupped his chin in his hand. "Then, what did you do?"

"I played *Mario Kart!*" JJ threw his arms up in excitement.

"Well, that's really cool." Eric stood back up.

"No, it's amazing!"

"Okay, it's amazing! Did you play with your aunt?"

"Yes, I played with Aunt Kay and Stef, but I am too fast for them! They don't know how to do shortcuts."

"True!" Kay stepped forward and introduced herself and Stef. "I kept falling off the road!"

"You kept *falling* off the road?" Stef interjected. "I couldn't even *find* the road. Too many crazy characters kept zipping by!"

JJ laughed. "They're funny!"

Ben introduced himself and his family. "You know, I used to be a *Mario Kart* expert when I was younger."

"Really?" JJ asked, intrigue in his eyes.

"You bet." Ben slung an arm over Eric's shoulder. "Remember how I used to beat you at every race, big brother?"

"Ha, ha." Eric flicked Ben's arm off.

While Ben and JJ talked details about video games, the two families chatted with each other. Eric wrapped an arm around Leah's shoulders, pulling her close to his side. She slid her arm around his waist and looked up at him, filled with pure joy. Both families coming together was the most wonderful ending to a magnificent day.

Chapter Nine

"Mommy, today I sang the whole song! I know all the words, and Mr. Eric sang harmony. It was amazing!"

"Wow, JJ, that's amazing! You didn't mention that earlier. Thank you for telling me."

"Yeah, he said I gave him the strength to do it."

Leah chuckled at his matter-of-fact statement. She could picture Eric saying exactly that. "Oh, he did, huh?"

"Yeah. He makes me feel strong, too."

She instantly had tears in her eyes. "That's wonderful." She leaned over to hug him. "Night night, sweet face."

"I love you, Mommy."

"Love you too."

A couple of hours later, Leah had just settled into bed and was about to turn her light off, when JJ appeared in her doorway.

"Mommy, I don't feel good."

He looked very pale, with dark circles under his eyes, and leaned against the wall while he held his tummy. Leah got up and felt his forehead. *Hot*, she thought. "Okay, let's see if you can go to the bathroom." She helped him into the bathroom, then found the thermometer and took his temperature. One hundred and three. Leah filled a cup of water and told him to take small sips, then opened the medicine cabinet.

"I can't stand up anymore, Mommy."

"Okay, let me help you get back into bed." Once JJ sat on the bed, she handed him the cup of water. "Here, take one more sip of water before you lie down." She got him settled and put the cup of water on his nightstand. "I'll be right back."

Leah looked in the medicine cabinet and found the acetaminophen, only it had expired. She looked again, but couldn't find another bottle, and she didn't have any ibuprofen. "I'm usually better organized," she chided herself.

"Mommy, I'm cold!" JJ whined.

"Okay, I'm coming." She grabbed two blankets from the linen closet and went back to JJ. He was shivering. She put one blanket over him. "Is that better?"

"No."

She put the second blanket over him and tucked them under his chin. "How's that?"

"A little better."

"Okay, try to take some deep breaths so that you can feel the warmth. Close your eyes. I need to try to find some medicine for you." She turned out his light, but left his door open, as she went back to her room.

The first call Leah made was to the on-call pediatrician. "Please, please pick up," she mumbled to herself, but ended up leaving a message. Even though it was after eleven o'clock at night, and she knew Kay and Stef were the early-to-bed, early-to-rise type, she called them anyway. "No." Kay's phone went straight to voicemail. She dialed Stef's phone, but no luck.

Next on her contact list was Carolyn, who had two young children at home in addition to Zelia. Even though Carolyn's husband would be home, Leah didn't feel comfortable asking her to leave her house at that hour. Next was Debbie, but Leah knew that Debbie was in New York.

Next was Eric.

Leah hesitated for a moment, but then reminded herself that she needed the medicine to keep JJ's fever under control before it spiked further. "Okay, I guess I'm doing this," she said to herself, then tapped the call to connect.

"Leah?"

"Hi, Eric, I hope I didn't wake you. I'm so sorry for calling this late."

He sensed a hint of urgency in her voice. "It's okay, I wasn't asleep. Is something wrong?"

"JJ woke up with a high fever. He has the chills and can't settle back to sleep. I foolishly let the medicine expire. I can't believe I did that. Kay and Stef turn their phones off when they go to bed, so they didn't answer my call. Debbie is in New York. I…" She was near tears.

"How can I help?" Eric could hear her worry and was already out of his bed. He threw his pants on, while the phone was tucked between his ear and shoulder.

"I'm waiting to hear back from the doctor, but in the meantime, I need a bottle of children's acetaminophen or ibuprofen, the liquid kind, because he doesn't know how to swallow a pill. The medicine should help the fever from spiking dangerously high. I don't even know if there are any pharmacies open at night anymore. I'm sorry."

"I'll find one. Go back to JJ. I'll be there in thirty minutes."

"Thank you."

"Anytime." He disconnected the call and almost knocked Madelyn off her feet when he ran into the hallway.

Leah went back into JJ's room and saw that he had sat up. The blankets were pushed away, his shirt was off, and his cheeks were bright red. "I'm sweating, Mommy."

She sat next to him on the bed and handed him the cup of water. "It's important to stay hydrated. Take a sip. Does your body hurt anywhere?"

"No, but my tummy feels funny."

"Okay. Try to take another sip of water." Leah emptied the trash basket and moved it next to his bed, just in case. Then, she went to get a washcloth. The doctor called while she soaked the washcloth in cold water.

She sat with JJ and placed the cold, damp washcloth on his forehead. "Take another sip." Leah held the cup to his lips and slowly tilted it. Then, she heard the doorbell and looked at the time on her phone. Eric had arrived within fifteen minutes. "Eric's here. Hopefully he found medicine for you. Keep taking small sips." She handed JJ the cup then ran downstairs.

"Thank you so much, and I'm sorry you had to run out this late," she apologized, letting Eric in.

"I actually didn't have to go anywhere. I ran into Madelyn, almost literally, on her way to the bathroom. She's well-stocked for the baby and had two bottles of infant acetaminophen. She said it's the same as the children's, and she wants you to have this." Eric handed Leah the bottle as they went back upstairs.

"Yes, it's just a different dose, fifteen milliliters every four to six hours for JJ. Thank goodness." She quickly brought the medicine to JJ. "Here we go, JJ. Hopefully this will help you feel a little better."

"I love you, Mommy."

"I love you too, sweet face."

Eric popped his head into JJ's room. "Hey, buddy."

"I don't feel good, Mr. Eric."

"I know. Try to get some rest. I hope you feel better quickly."

"Mommy, can you stay with me?" JJ asked.

"Of course." Leah spread herself out next to him, cradling him close. He started to shiver again, so she removed the washcloth and put his pajama top back on. After a while, JJ finally fell asleep. She carefully got out of the bed and laid his head on the pillow, then covered him with the blankets.

Leah walked into the living room and found Eric sitting in a corner of the couch, his legs extended on the coffee table. He had taken his sneakers off and put a throw pillow on the table. His feet rested on the pillow, crossed at the ankles, socks loosened around his toes. His arms were crossed over his chest, and his head rested on another throw pillow. He was wearing sweats, and his eyes were closed, a few stray locks of hair falling onto his forehead. Eric looked like he was at home, in her home. The glimmer that sparkled inside her grew.

The floor creaked when Leah stepped forward, and he opened his eyes. "Oh, I'm sorry," she said. "I thought you were asleep."

"Nope, I'm awake, just resting. How's JJ?"

"He's finally asleep." She looked at the time on her phone: almost one o'clock in the morning. "For whatever reason, I thought you'd left after you saw JJ."

"I wanted to wait for you."

"Oh, Eric, that wasn't—"

"Necessary?" he finished. "I know, but I'm worried about JJ, too. I want to be here for you, Leah." He sat up straight and tapped the couch next to himself. Leah's eyes were red and puffy from worry and fatigue, and all he wanted at that moment was to hold her.

Leah sat down next to him, and when he wrapped his arm around her, she relaxed her head onto his shoulder. "I didn't mean to worry you. I've been through fevers countless times before. JJ and I have overcome so many hurdles over the years that a fever seems like nothing in comparison. I've just never been so careless as to let the medicine expire, and it scared me to think of what could happen to him if his fever spiked higher."

"You're human, Leah. I'm sure every parent, at some point, has let something expire. Your fears are completely understandable. I can only imagine what the two of you have been through, but I'm here for you if you ever want to talk about anything. I'm so glad you called me. Did you hear back from the doctor?"

"I appreciate your support," she replied. "Yes, the doctor said that if the acetaminophen helps to bring the fever down, then just keep doing what I'm doing, make sure he's hydrated, is able to use the bathroom, and that he rests. I only need to bring JJ in if the fever goes up, or if he develops other symptoms…which reminds me, I need to set an alarm on my phone to call the absent line at JJ's school in the morning and check his temperature at that point." Leah set the alarm, then plugged her phone into the charging station on the side table at the other end of the couch.

She glanced over her shoulder at Eric, finding comfort in his smile. *He was here for JJ and me*, she thought, and her heart smiled. *Though… for how long? He could find a new adventure at any moment and be off traveling again. JJ's bonded with Eric; he would be devastated if Eric were to leave. And my heart couldn't bear being broken again.* She rubbed her throbbing temples, reasoning that fatigue had flashed those vulnerabilities before her.

When Leah looked at him again, he opened his arms. She pushed away the image of heartache that had crept into her head and replaced it with hope. At least for that night, she didn't want him to leave. She glided back down the couch and into his arms. "Thank you, again, Eric. It's the middle of the night now. You're welcome to stay, if you don't mind sleeping on the couch?"

"I'm tired and will gratefully accept your offer. The couch is perfectly fine."

Leah nodded and stood. "I'll get you a bigger pillow and warmer blanket. And as soon as I get the chance, I'll get another bottle of medicine for Madelyn."

"No need to get anything for me, I'm already comfortable, and Madelyn won't accept it. She insisted that you keep it."

Leah sat back down and looked at Eric, beholden. "I have to do something in return, for Madelyn and for you."

He brushed her hair off her face, then held her hands. "Leah, you give back to everyone on a daily basis, in ways I don't think you're aware of. If you really want to do something for Madelyn, call or text her. I'll give you her number. She'd love to hear from you and to know how JJ is doing. For me, let me in. Let me hold you tonight."

"I…I don't know what to say." She lowered her head.

"Say what you feel."

Leah closed her eyes, but she couldn't ignore the pool of emotion welling within her again. It was strong. The possibility of Eric's departure had been washed away, and all that was left in its wake, was his presence. She had to jump in. Leah opened her eyes, looking deeply into his.

"I want you to hold me," she said. "Please, hold me."

Eric shifted back against the couch, propped his feet back up on the pillow, and pulled her close to his side. Leah tucked her legs up onto the couch and snuggled into him, her head resting on his chest along with the palm of her hand. She was asleep almost instantly.

With his free hand, Eric reached over his head to the blanket that was draped over the back of the couch. He covered Leah with it, then closed his eyes and drifted to sleep.

* * *

A cheerful piano melody echoed from Leah's phone, the sound filling the living room. Leah, in a state of somnolence, scooted down the couch to her phone. She turned the alarm off and called the school to report JJ absent. Then, she slid back over to Eric, laid her head on his lap, and went back to sleep.

Eric chuckled to himself as he watched the half-asleep exchange. "You are something else, Leah Preston," he whispered. He gently lifted Leah's head so he could stand up, then swiftly replaced his legs with the pillow. She curled herself up, sighing as sleep took over. He covered her back up with the blanket, then he went to check on JJ.

As Eric peeked into JJ's room, he saw the young boy stir and rub his eyes in an effort to wake up. Eric felt content that he was able to experience that moment with JJ. So as not to startle JJ, he spoke softly, "Good morning, JJ."

JJ half opened his eyes, and looked at his doorway. "Oh, Mr. Eric, did you sleep over? Where's Mommy?"

"Yes, I slept on the couch. I hope that's okay with you. Your mom is still sleeping, and I didn't want to wake her up. How are you feeling?"

"I'm happy that you are here, Mr. Eric. I don't know how I feel."

"Well, I'm going to help you get up and into the bathroom, so we can figure out how you're doing. Okay?"

"Okay."

* * *

Leah woke to the bold scent of coffee wafting through the living room. As she walked into the kitchen, she saw Eric sitting at the table with a coffee mug in his hands. Papers were scattered on the table, and his intense focus was on one document. Then, she looked over at the coffee pot, next to the microwave, and noticed the time on its display.

"No, no, no!" she blurted out.

Eric's coffee sloshed in its mug as he was startled. "Leah, I didn't see you there! What is it?"

"I slept through my alarm! I was supposed to call the school and check on JJ two hours ago!" She turned, heading toward JJ's room.

Eric quickly went after her. "Shh, he's asleep." Eric spoke quietly, bringing her back into the kitchen. "You already called the school, and went right back to sleep. I took care of JJ," he explained, clearing his paperwork off the table.

"I did? You did?" With bewilderment, Leah pointed to herself, then to him.

Eric stopped what he was doing and looked at her. Aside from confusion, Leah's eyes were bright and rested. He realized that, since he had arrived the night before, he hadn't had a chance to fully digest her appearance. She was covered in a pastel pink, one-piece fleece pajama, her feet inside of plush gray socks. The pajama's zipper ran down the length of her body, from the top of her chest to her...and her hair was mussed around her face, the ponytail barely hanging on. Her image, so adorable yet so alluring at the same time, caused him to lose his breath.

He brushed a hand through his hair, trying to redirect himself back to the conversation. "Um, yeah. You did, and I did. I think I remembered everything you had said. JJ used the bathroom and drank a cup of water. I found the thermometer in the bathroom and took his temperature. It had gone down to one hundred point six. He said that he felt better, but told me to tell you that he isn't all the way better. We read *Library Lion*, and then he fell back asleep."

Leah smiled softly. "Thank you so much for taking such good care of him. I'm glad to hear he's a little better. *Library Lion* is our favorite book."

"Yeah, he told me that. You like cream in your coffee, right?" Eric pulled down a mug for her.

She dropped onto a chair, holding her head in her hand. "You must think I'm a terrible mother. First, I let the medicine expire, and *then* I fall asleep when I should be taking care of my sick son."

"On the contrary," Eric answered. "I've seen you in action with JJ multiple times over the last couple of weeks. You're a devoted, loving mom. Clearly, you were exhausted. I think your subconscious allowed you to sleep because it told you there was someone else here to help you."

Leah looked at him and laughed. "So, now your talents include being able to hear my subconscious speak?"

Her laugh was infectious. "Yes, I believe its exact words were: 'Sleep until your worries are none, a handsome man will take care of you and your son.'" He performed as though he were in a Shakespearean play.

"Bravo!" She gave him a standing ovation. "I have to agree with my subconscious! Seriously, though, thank you for all that you've done for JJ and me."

"Anytime. How about that coffee?"

"Thanks. Yes, a little bit of cream, please," she replied. "I'm going to take a quick peek at JJ, and before I forget, I need to call Carolyn to make sure Zelia can cover my classes today and tomorrow. JJ will need to stay home again, since his temperature hasn't yet returned to normal. I'll be back in just a few minutes."

"Take your time."

When Leah returned to the kitchen, she noticed that Eric had gone into the living room and sat on a chair, paperwork on his lap and a coffee mug in his hand. She sat on the couch, picked up the mug that he had put on the coffee table for her and took a sip. "Eric, you can go to work. I have things under control now."

"I had some paperwork in the car, so fortunately I've been able to get a little work done here. As long as I'm at Bridge of Music before my first lesson, then I'll be fine," he reassured her. "My years of travel taught me to always keep a clean set of clothes in the car, as well. I'd like to take a shower before I go, if that's okay?"

"Absolutely! I'll get you a towel."

"Leah, before you do that, there is something that has been on my mind for a while that I would like to talk to you about." He stacked his paperwork on the floor and moved from the chair to next to her on the couch.

Leah put her mug on the table and faced him. Eric had become solemn, and she wasn't quite sure how to respond, other than, "Okay."

"I feel that we have a connection, and I believe that you feel it too," he began. "I'd like to grow what we've started, though I don't want to make you uncomfortable, or push you to talk about—"

Leah placed her hands over his, interrupting him. She knew it was time that she told him her story.

"Eric, yes," she said. "I feel it too. I want you to know what happened in my past. Though it was extremely painful, I am where I am now because I worked hard to get through it and moved forward." She lowered her head and took a deep breath.

"Daniel happened to me." Leah looked back up at Eric. "JJ's father." She paused and took another breath. "We were together for eight years. I thought we were in love. We'd been living together for quite some time, but when I brought up marriage, he told me that we had plenty of time to think about that. Then, my parents became ill and passed, one right after the other." She crossed over to the television stand and picked up a framed photograph, gently touching the image of her parents' faces. Then, Leah hugged the frame for a moment and put it back.

"It was a rough few years for Kay and me, and because of that, things with Daniel remained status quo. He seemed happy, and I was too preoccupied with my family to bring up marriage again. Soon after Kay and I settled my parents' estate, I thought that it would be okay to allow myself to breathe a little…and that's when I became pregnant." She sat back down next to Eric and continued, looking down at her hands. "Daniel told me…" Leah closed her eyes. *I'm not going to shed any more tears over Daniel*, she reminded herself. "Daniel told me that he didn't want the responsibility. He didn't want to make a permanent commitment to me, and he didn't want the baby. He left me."

She opened her eyes and looked at Eric, afraid that she would see judgment or pity in his gaze…but all she saw was affection. "I was thirty-one years old, pregnant, and terrified. I was freelancing in the public schools, teaching dance and movement workshops, but I wasn't earning enough to afford an apartment on my own. I had to move in with Kay and Stef. Lydia created a job for me so that I could have health insurance, and taught me everything I know about business management. The residents of the town came together and donated everything I'd need for the baby. As soon as JJ was born and I saw him, held him, I knew what true love really meant. My heart was full. Because Daniel wasn't there to sign JJ's birth certificate, I became his sole legal parent. I gave him my name, Preston, and was able to close the door on my hurt and anger over Daniel."

Leah continued, "Lydia noticed JJ's delayed development, and she set me up with a neurologist and early intervention. Nicole, Kay, and Stef helped with babysitting and have continued to do so. I'd met Carolyn through the schools, when Zelia, who enjoyed my workshops, was little. Carolyn rallied with several other families to try and convince me to open my own dance studio. I didn't know how I'd be able to make that possible, and at the same time, I was becoming overwhelmed by JJ's diagnosis and all that it entailed. That was when Debbie stepped in, and you know what she did for JJ and me. It took time, but eventually, I built up sufficient student enrollment and was able to make ends meet. I've had continued support from everyone in the town, and I'm immensely grateful and determined to give back. JJ has never asked about his father. I don't know if it's because he's always been surrounded by people who love him, or if it just hasn't occurred to him. I know, at some point, I'm going to have to tell JJ about Daniel, and if he chooses to try to find him, I'll have to let him, as hard as that will be for me…"

Leah trailed off and again looked down into her hands.

Eric lifted her chin, looking into her golden depths. He knew the sparkle hid somewhere within.

"Leah, I am truly sorry about the loss of your parents," he said. "I'm sure they are watching over you and JJ with pride. I'm appalled by the actions of the man who did that to you. I can't fathom how the guy was able to turn his back on you, on his own son. My admiration for you, my *awe* of you, just grew tenfold. Your strength, your kindness…you're inspiring." Eric took the ponytail holder out of her hair, smoothing the strands around her face and behind her shoulders. "And you're incredibly beautiful."

Overcome with emotion, Leah threw her arms around Eric's neck and he gently embraced her, one arm around her waist, the other hand behind her head. "Tighter," she requested. He stood with her, pulling her in close to him.

As he held her, she felt her heart open, love floating in. She sighed peacefully, as she laid her head on his chest and let her hands drift down around his waist. As he gently rocked her, she realized that there was something she needed to know about him. She looked up into his eyes, "It's your turn, now."

He furrowed his brow. "My turn?"

"Yes, I have a question for you. Well, I guess I have two questions. Have you ever been in a committed relationship? JJ once asked what home means to you, and while your reaction was comical at the time, I have wondered… what really is your answer to that question?"

Leah had willingly bared herself to him and she had done so honestly. She deserved the same from him. Eric brushed a hand through his hair. "The root of both your questions stems from my childhood. I was privileged to grow up in a very loving and supportive home. My parents are high school sweethearts. They married young, had me when they were young, and even when they quarreled, they were still able to show their love for each other. Ben came ten years after me. Madelyn's parents lived a few houses down from us, and when Madelyn's mom became pregnant with her only two months after my mom became pregnant with Ben, the two women bonded. I've joked that Ben and Madelyn fell in love in the womb, but they really have been together their entire lives. My parents found their sense of belonging with each other, and Ben found his with Madelyn. I wanted to find that for myself. I started to travel and found music, found passion in my work, and with the kids. I've dated many women along the way, but I've never found anyone who touched my heart or made me feel that sense of belonging, of home. Until…"

The bright sparkle in Leah's eyes came out of hiding, and Eric became lost in her aureate brilliance. He gently stroked the length of her hair, then her cheek, as he leaned closer to her.

"Until?" she whispered, closing her eyes and angling her head up to meet him.

"You," he breathed. His lips had barely brushed hers, when they were startled.

"Mommy!" JJ yelled out from his room.

Eric let out his breath, tilting his head so that his forehead rested against hers. "You should go to him."

Leah stepped back, touched his cheek, and smiled softly. Then, she went to JJ's room.

"JJ, what's wrong?" she asked.

"Mommy!" He opened his arms, relief in his eyes.

Leah went over to JJ's bed and sat down to hug him. "Are you feeling worse?"

"I got scared when I woke up and you weren't here, because you weren't here earlier."

"Oh, I'm sorry, I didn't mean to scare you. I was sleeping earlier. I know you're used to seeing me when you wake up. I'm awake now, and I'm here. Do you feel better?"

"Yeah. Mr. Eric was here before."

"Were you happy to see him?"

"Yeah, but I missed you."

"Love you." She stood up to look at him. "You look like you're better, but let's go take your temperature to make sure."

A few minutes later, JJ ran ahead of Leah into the kitchen. "Mr. Eric, you're still here!"

Eric had the eggs scrambled and poured them into the pan; bread was in the toaster. "Just for a little while longer. I have to go to work soon. Are you feeling better?"

"Yeah, my temperature is almost normal. Mommy says that I have to stay home tomorrow, but then I can go back to school."

"I'm very happy to hear that!"

"JJ, do you think you could try to eat some soup and crackers?" When Leah walked into the kitchen, her heart smiled at the domestic scene of Eric by the stove, the dish towel over his shoulder.

"Okay, Mommy."

She put the pot of soup onto the stove, next to Eric's pan. "So, you can cook, too?"

He swung the dish towel around her waist, keeping a grip on it with both hands. "Out of necessity. When I was traveling, it was better to learn some basics rather than always eating out, nothing fancy. I made enough for you, but unfortunately, you will be stuck with the clean-up, because I do need to get to work." He twirled the dish towel and handed it to her.

"You're very sweet, thank you, and no worries about the clean-up."

JJ seemed more like himself as he chatted away while they ate. Leah was relieved that the worst was over.

"I'm sorry to have to cut this short." Eric stood once he had finished his plate. "Leah, I have just enough time to grab a quick shower, if that's okay?"

"Sure, go ahead. The towels are still in the dryer, so I'll get one for you. JJ, try to drink a little more of the soup before it gets cold. I'll be right back, okay?"

"Okay, Mommy."

Leah pulled a towel out of the dryer, then knocked on the bathroom door. "Eric, I have a towel…oh!"

When Eric opened the door, she was mesmerized by the sight of him. His shirt was already off, and he was impressively solid: strong and broad across the shoulders and arms, and temptingly sculpted along the chest and waist.

"Thanks." He tried to take the towel, but she had it hugged tightly to her. He took a step toward her and flicked the zipper on her pajama, then slowly began to unzip. "Did you want to join me?" he proposed, with a deep rasp in his voice.

Yes! Leah's mind screamed. She was momentarily frozen, before reason stepped in. Playfully swatting his hand away, she zipped herself back up. "No, no." She pushed the towel at him and quickly went back to the kitchen. Eric chuckled as he watched her go.

Once he was finished in the bathroom, Eric gathered his sweats and paperwork, then said goodbye to JJ, who was on the couch, engrossed in the movie playing on the TV.

As Eric walked downstairs with Leah, an ingenious image envisaged itself. "It's occurred to me that, with all the time we've spent together, I have yet to take you on a proper date. I'd like to rectify that." At the door, he turned to her and held her hands. "Leah, would you do me the honor of being my date this Friday evening?"

"I would love to, Eric!"

"I'll take care of all the details. All you need to do is be ready by eight."

"I'm looking forward to it!"

"You've made me a very happy man."

The first phone call Eric made once he walked out the door was to Kay's Canines.

* * *

Later that day, after watching a movie with JJ, Leah sat at the kitchen table and made a couple of phone calls. She typed in the number that Eric had given her and tapped send to connect the call.

"Hello?" a female voice answered.

"Hi, Madelyn! It's Leah."

"Hi! Hold on, let me add you as a contact before I forget," she said. "Okay, hi! How's JJ?"

"He's doing so much better, thanks to you! The medicine you gave me did bring the fever down and allowed him to rest. Temp is almost back to normal."

"That's great! What a relief, huh? I'm glad I was overstocked for the baby."

"How are you doing? Can I get you anything?"

"My hospital bag is packed. Could be any day now. I'm very uncomfortable! I have to sleep in the recliner chair, and Ben has to pull me up! But, thanks, I'm all set. I don't need anything right now."

"Well, if you ever do need anything at all, I hope you know you can call me. It will all be worth it as soon as the doctor puts the baby in your arms. Trust me, it's a feeling like no other."

"And now you've made me cry! My hormones!"

Leah laughed. "Would you mind adding me to your list of people to notify when the baby comes?"

"You already are. Eric will definitely call you. I have to run to the bathroom, well, if only I *could* run! Anyway, thanks for calling!"

"Take care, and thank you again for the medicine!" Leah disconnected the call, thankful for a new friend and excited to shop for a baby gift in the near future.

She checked on JJ, made sure he drank some water, and gave him one more dose of medicine. Then, he plopped down on the couch with his head on the armrest and pulled the blanket over himself. Leah put another movie into the DVD player and went back into the kitchen.

After she finally had a chance to clear the dishes from breakfast, she called Kay. Barks bellowed through the phone as soon as the call connected.

"Hey! Sorry about that. I was handing over Bentley to his owner."

"I had a feeling you were with one of the dogs," Leah said. "Is this an okay time to talk for a minute?"

"I have a few minutes before I need to start bathing my next dog. What's up?"

"I'm wondering if you and Stef can watch JJ Friday night?"

"Why, what's going on?"

"Eric asked me on a date!"

"He asked her on a date!" Kay yelled through the glass to Stef.

"Finally!" Stef yelled back, followed by a chorus of barks.

Leah laughed. "So does that mean you both can watch JJ?"

"Actually, I don't think we can," Kay responded, then yelled to Stef. "What is it again that we have Friday night?" she asked, even though she already knew what they would be busy with.

"Oh, of course, put it on me to say," Stef shot back. "It's, um, the grooming convention."

"Right. We have a grooming convention," Kay repeated to Leah.

"Okay. You've never mentioned conventions before."

"Well, there's a first time for everything, right? Did Eric tell you anything about the date?"

"No, but he said he'd take care of all the details. I'm excited and nervous. I haven't been on a date in a very long time."

"Don't think about it, just enjoy it."

"You're right, I will!"

"I need to go to my next dog now. I'm sure you can find someone else to watch JJ, though."

"I'll make some calls. Enjoy your convention."

"Yep, right. Love you!"

"Love you, too!"

Leah joined JJ on the couch to watch the movie and quickly took his temperature. Back to normal, thank goodness. While they snuggled, Leah's phone chimed. It was Nicole calling in, so Leah got up and walked out of the living room as she answered the call. "Hi, Nicole!"

"Hi! How are you?"

"Better, now. JJ had a high fever last night, but thankfully it was short-lived."

"Oh, no! I'm glad he's doing better. The girls are wondering if they can hang out with JJ this Friday night?"

"Aren't they in school right now?"

"Of course, yes, yes they are. They asked me before they left this morning and I've been crazy busy, you know, so I didn't have a chance to call you until now."

"Gotcha. Well, as it turns out, I am in need of someone to watch JJ Friday night, so it's great they're available. Can they be here by seven-thirty?"

"Yes, they can, and don't worry about feeding them. I'll make sure they eat before I bring them over. They're capable of feeding JJ when he gets hungry for dinner."

"Okay, thank you, but I'm happy to order a pizza. How late can they stay?"

"No need for the pizza this time, really," Nicole said. "They can stay as late as you need. They'll text me when they're ready for me to pick them up. What are you doing Friday night?" Nicole feigned unawareness, because Eric had already told her the plan and had asked if the girls were available.

"I have a date with Eric!"

"How exciting! I'm so happy for you."

"I don't even know if I have anything to wear," Leah said, realization setting in. More often than not, she wore her dance clothes.

"I'll come over Friday morning after I drop the girls off at school. If there isn't anything in your closet, we'll go shopping!"

"Great, thanks, see you then!"

Chapter Ten

By Friday morning, JJ was back in school, and Leah enjoyed some quality time with her friend. Even though the wind knocked on her window and raindrops decorated the outer pane, Leah felt sunny and was filled with an excited anticipation of what the evening would hold.

"I have black and gray dress pants." Leah pulled them out of her closet, while Nicole sat on the bed.

Nicole scrunched her nose. "You don't have any dresses?"

"I have less than a handful of dresses, but they're kind of summery."

"What's in the garment bag?"

"Oh, that's for the winter concert."

"Can I take a look?" Nicole walked over to where it hung on the door and unzipped the bag. "Leah, this is gorgeous!"

"It really is." Leah gently lifted the dress out of the bag so that Nicole could see it in full. "Pauline had a huge sale at her dress shop just after the new year, and I was fortunate to have found this." She carefully tucked it back in the bag.

Nicole pulled out a dress from the closet, then put it back. "I should tell Rebecca to go see Pauline about a job. She definitely has an interest in fashion design. Lori, though, has an interest in web design, which I know nothing about. I'd have to read an instructional book to understand that language!"

"Yeah, I'm not tech savvy either. Lori can help me with the studio's website anytime!" Leah replied. "And that's a good idea for Rebecca. I think Pauline was looking for assistance in the alterations department."

"I'll let the girls know, but not tonight. You are going to focus on having fun and romance!" Nicole pulled out a black slip dress with a delicate floral overlay. "Here, see if this one still fits."

Leah put the dress on and examined herself in the full-length mirror, swiveling from one direction to the other. It hugged her curves attractively, with a V-neckline in the front and the back, attached to flutter sleeves over her shoulders. The floral overlay added a softness around her thighs and knees.

"That's the one!" Nicole clapped her hands together.

"I agree. I have the freshwater pearl necklace and bracelet that my mother gave me. They'll go perfect with this." Leah took off the dress and hung it outside her closet.

"Great!" said Nicole. "Now, let's go get bagels, then shop for gifts for Eric's soon-to-be nephew!"

"That's a plan!" Leah linked arms with Nicole as they left the apartment.

* * *

"You look pretty, Mommy!" JJ exclaimed.

"Thank you, my sweet face!"

"What's a date?"

"It's when two people who really like each other have a special time together." Leah looked at JJ, who was curled up in her bed. "Are you okay with my having a date with Eric?"

"Yes, Mommy. Are you going to marry him?"

"Oh, getting married is a big step. This is our first date, so let's see how it goes, okay?"

"Okay, Mommy," he replied. "If you do get married one day, can Mr. Eric be my daddy?"

Leah had not expected that. She hugged JJ tightly, resting her head on his. "JJ, you do have a daddy, but he chose to move away a long time ago, and I don't know where he is."

"Why did he move away, Mommy?"

"He moved away because that's what he thought would be best." Tears stung her eyes, not for Daniel, but for JJ. She could not tell JJ that his father hadn't wanted him.

"What is his name?"

"His name is Daniel."

"Did I ever meet Daniel?"

"No, you've never met him."

JJ became silent and fidgeted with Leah's hair. She rubbed his back, holding him close. "How are you feeling, JJ? Do you have any other questions?"

"I feel good, Mommy, because you didn't move away," he said. "I don't have any more questions."

"I'm not going anywhere. You know how much I love you and that you mean everything to me, right?"

"I love you, too, Mommy."

"And you know that there are so many people here who you know and who love you very much."

"I know, Mommy. I don't want a daddy that I've never met. I want to choose Mr. Eric."

"I'll keep that in mind," Leah said. "For now, though, I just want you to enjoy your lessons with him, enjoy spending time with him, and focus on that, okay?" She was actually relieved that JJ knew about Daniel. Leah had been fearful of broaching the topic, but she realized that JJ's reaction was in accordance with how his autistic brain worked. He best understood information that was concrete, rather than abstract. He wanted what was already familiar to him, rather than unknown scenarios of the future or what could have been from the past. Though, if JJ ever wanted to know more about Daniel, she would be there for him. She also sent a wish out into the universe, hoping that Eric would want to stay. JJ had a close bond with Eric, as did she, and if Eric were to leave, two hearts would break.

"Okay, Mommy."

"Good. Now, I need to finish getting ready, and I think Lori and Rebecca have your dinner ready, so go into the kitchen and eat, okay?"

"Okay, Mommy." JJ hopped out of her bed and ran toward the kitchen.

Leah needed to take a quiet moment of reflection. She also wanted to enjoy her time with Eric, and she took a few slow, deep breaths, trying to focus on just that. With her eyes closed, she smiled as she exhaled, feeling renewed by the notion that her heart did have more room to give, and to receive.

She decided to leave her hair down long in the back, with the front strands rolled away from her face and clipped loosely at the back of her head. As Leah adjusted the hair clip, Lori knocked on her bedroom door. "Ms. Preston, Mr. Hynes is here. I let him in."

"Thank you, Lori. I'm coming." With one final look at herself in the mirror, she smoothed her hands down her dress and nodded her head.

When Leah stepped into the hallway, her breath caught at the sight of Eric's ravishingly masculine appearance. His hands were in the pockets of his dark navy pants, stance wide and evenly-centered. He wore a contrasting light blue shirt, open at the collar, sleeves rolled up onto his forearms, the tails tucked into his pants, showcasing his well-defined waist. His hair was brushed neatly back, though she predicted that those locks would become messed onto his forehead.

Leah felt a rush filling her from her toes, which then swirled around her and floated her down the hallway. She eyed Eric as he shifted his weight and leaned his head to one side, bringing a hand up to tap his heart. Her bright golden gaze met his dark flowing sea, and Leah tilted her head, offering him a soft, sideways smile and one slow flutter of her lashes.

When she reached him, her palms floated over his chest and under his collar. "Hi," she sighed.

Eric's heart roared in his chest, its pulse permeating through him to his core. He melted from the touch of the enchantress before him. He placed his hands over hers and felt her warmth; only then was he certain that she was truly there and not merely a dream. He didn't take his eyes off Leah as he skimmed his thumbs over her palms, then extended his arms, gliding her back, then twirling her in close again. "You take my breath away," he whispered softly, deeply.

Neither Leah, nor Eric noticed the three young faces peeking around the corner from the kitchen, but they heard the chorus of giggles.

"Bye, kids." Eric projected his voice as he put an arm around Leah's waist and led her out the door.

Over her shoulder, Leah acknowledged them. "Love you, JJ. Thanks, girls." On their way downstairs, she gently ran her fingers along Eric's forearm. "You look incredible, Eric."

"And you, Leah, are enchanting."

"Oh!" She stopped. "I forgot my coat!"

When she started to head back upstairs, he kept moving her forward. "You won't need it."

"In January?"

Eric smiled at her as he opened the back door to the dance studio. "Welcome, Mademoiselle, to your little piece of France." He spoke with a French accent as he guided her through the door.

Leah was enraptured by all that charged her senses. She felt as though she had been teleported to a sidewalk cafe in Paris, as she slowly strolled to the center of the room and looked around.

Romantic French melodies softly filled the air. The mirror that lined one wall of the studio was covered by a tapestry of the

Eiffel Tower overlooking the Seine River at night; the gleaming lights of the Eiffel Tower cast sparkling shadows over the water. Along the opposite wall were tables elegantly decorated with yellow linen, which was also draped over the ballet barre. Atop the tables sat a row of potted white lilies. Candles bordered the floor of the entire room, bringing life and movement as they illuminated the space with dancing flames.

In the center of it all was a small, round table with two chairs placed opposite one another. Next to the round table sat a trolley with covered food warmers, emanating an aromatic mixture of vegetables, herbs, thyme, sweet vanilla, and rich coffee. All signs of her dance studio had been expertly hidden.

Leah closed her eyes and slowly spun around, taking in the authenticity of Paris. When she opened her eyes, she looked over her shoulder to find Eric behind her. She turned to him and held his hands.

"How did you..." Emotion carried her into his arms. "Thank you so much." Then, she opened her arms so that she stood next to him, but kept ahold of one of his hands. As she admired the scene again, she exclaimed, "This is absolutely magical!"

"I'm completely spellbound," Eric agreed, though he wasn't looking around the room. His eyes had been on Leah the entire time, entranced by her joy and awe. He offered her a chair. "Mademoiselle."

"Thank you, kind sir."

With a French accent, he presented the contents on the food trolley. "For dinner, we have French roasted chicken, ratatouille, French baguette, crème brulée, and French espresso."

"This is all excitingly novel for me!"

"You have never experienced these delicacies?"

She laughed at his continued impression of a French server. "No, sir, I have not."

"Then you are in for a fabulous treat." Eric prepared a plate for her, then for himself, before joining her at the table.

Leah tried the ratatouille first. "Wow!"

"It's good, right? I know you like vegetables."

"It's *so* beyond good! I have no words." She relished in more. "Okay, Eric, how on earth did you do all of this?"

"Magic."

She blinked, almost believing him. At least, she wanted to believe.

He laughed heartily. "The expression on your face is priceless!" He reached out to stroke her cheek, and her eyes softened. "I had some help pulling this off."

"Oh, Kay and Stef, of course! They're the only ones, other than me, who have a key to the studio." *Well, that explains their grooming convention*, she realized.

"Yes, they've been very helpful."

"Where'd you find the dinner?"

"I have an old friend who went to culinary school in France, then came back here to open a French-style café in Brookline. I contacted him, and he was happy to help. He also set me up with the florist, as well as a place where I could find the tapestry. I'll definitely take you to his café. It's quite the experience, and I'm confident you'd enjoy it. Tonight, though, I wanted to create this scene for you… and, if I'm being honest, I didn't want to share you with anyone else this time."

"The café sounds lovely," Leah said. "It means so much to me that you did all this for me! It's incredibly romantic and truly magical."

"Paris is the most romantic city in the world. One day, I want to go back there, but only with you. I want to see the city through your eyes, to stand with you by the Eiffel Tower, to go on a dinner cruise along the Seine, to walk across Pont des Arts, to find hidden treasures along the cobblestone streets and through the gardens…"

The candlelight highlighted Leah's features in the most seductive of ways, as did the dreamy look in her eyes as she intently listened to him. Eric had to have her in his arms. "May I have this dance?" he asked. He stood and offered his hand.

"Yes." She delicately placed her hand in his and joined him.

As Eric wrapped an arm around her, Leah draped hers around his shoulder. Her body molded with his, and he held her other hand against his heart. The rhythm of the melodies became theirs as they swayed together. His beard caressed her cheek as he leaned into her, and they both closed their eyes, reveling in the warmth that encompassed them.

Eric lifted her arm and sent Leah under it in a pivot, extended his arms, then spun her back to him in a full turn so that her back leaned against his chest. His arms were crossed over hers, in front of her.

She tilted her head back with a smile. "You can dance! Your talents do not cease, Eric Hynes."

He uncurled her, so that she was once again facing him. "That's my only move, but I'm pleased that you liked it."

"You're too modest. That's not your only move." Leah twirled her fingers through his hair until the locks ended up on his forehead, then gently brushed the backs of her fingers along his beard. "You, Eric, have made me feel things I never dreamed I could. I admire your empathy and awareness of others. You are intelligent and creative." She paused to dip into his sea.

"Oh, that's all?" He beamed at her.

"You make me laugh!" And she did so. "You make me feel safe. I admire your strength of mind. All that you are makes you incredibly...sexy." She lowered her gaze to his lips, then back to his eyes, in which waves billowed and crashed.

"You think I'm sexy?" Eric's deep, throaty voice was filled with desire, as he placed her hand over his heart. Then, he rubbed his hand up Leah's arm and under her wispy sleeve, squeezing her shoulder.

"Incredibly," she responded, barely a whisper, while she held his gaze and trailed a finger around his ear and down the side of his neck.

The golden specks in Leah's eyes were blindingly bright. Eric lowered his head close to hers and nuzzled one side of her face, then the other, then paused, inches from her mouth. Their breath intertwined, and her eyes slowly closed, while he gently stroked his fingers around her shoulder to the underside of her arm, then down the side of her breast. He caught her sigh as his lips met hers.

Heat electrified Leah's entire being as she rose onto her toes, wrapping her arms around his neck. Then, she melted into him, as he deepened the kiss.

Eric lifted her closer against him, leaning over her. With one arm gripped tightly around her, his other slid up her back, hand wrapping in her hair. Leah was so delicate, so soft, and at the same time extremely responsive. He tasted her sweetness, and was overcome by sensations he had never before experienced. He didn't think he would ever be able to get enough of her, but eventually, he softened the kiss and lowered her down, gently dancing his fingers along her arms. He leaned his forehead against hers, but kept his eyes closed.

"That was magical," Eric said softly.

Leah smoothed her palms across his chest, keeping her eyes closed as well. "Yes. Yes, that was most definitely magical." She tried to recover her breath, though her body still tingled, as she rested her head on his chest and embraced him. Eric held her and rocked her to the melodies that he was once again able to hear.

While Leah continued to rest on him, she admitted, "I really want to finish eating, now."

He chuckled. "Absolutely."

They held their embrace for another silent moment, then settled back at the table.

"These bouquets of lilies are not only gorgeous, but they're also my favorite flower." While she enjoyed her meal, Leah admired the blooms set on the table.

"Actually, I already knew that." Eric smiled confidently as he popped a piece of the chicken into his mouth.

"Of course you did. Okay, then, what's your favorite flower?"

"I have to say, I've never really thought about having a particular preference for one flower over another. However, if lilies are your favorite, then they're my favorite as well." Eric went over to the potted flowers, pulled out a bloom, and shortened its stem. Before sitting back down, he tucked the bloom inside the hair clip at the back of her head. "I agree with you. It's gorgeous."

"You're very sweet, thank you. I guess this means that you already know my favorite color is yellow?"

"Indeed."

"Do you have a favorite color?"

"I favor blue." He reached out to hold her hand, rolling his thumb across her bracelet. "What gem is this?"

Leah touched her necklace. "Both the bracelet and necklace are freshwater pearls. My mother gave them to me when I was young. They're elegant, my favorite."

"Noted. They're beautiful."

"I would love to hear more about your time in Paris," she continued. "What did you enjoy the most?"

"The people, not only in the touristy spots, but also in the places that are part of Parisian daily life. There are many markets and parks to stroll through, where passersby are always acknowledged with '*bonjour*' or '*bonne journée,*' 'good day.' There's one market, in particular, that I found, which became my favorite: the Marché d'Aligre in the twelfth arrondissement, or 'district,' of Paris. The street there is lined with outdoor stalls of vendors from local farms. Just the view itself is picturesque, with a plethora of colors from the fruits and vegetables on display. Sweet fragrance swirls through the air, almost intoxicating, and shouts from vendors can be heard in all directions, each one trying to convince shoppers to stop by their stall. Once you stop, they engage you in conversation, offering a friendly smile. They're interested in getting to know you, and happy to share their techniques of growing quality produce. Ultimately, they're able to expertly make a recommendation as to which of their staples will suit you best. I greatly enjoyed my visits there…the sights, sounds, smells, and especially the people. It was always a pleasure talking with the vendors and hearing their stories. Every time, I left the market with more purchases than I had intended!"

Eric laughed in fond remembrance. "But my favorite aspects of this market were the two stalls at the back corner of the street, where, past the sweet aromas from the other vendors, there was the scent of freshly-baked bread. Not only did the scent catch my attention, but so did the vendor. She never shouted, but instead opened her arms, with a sway of her wrists and a twinkle in her eyes. Madame Anais is a stout, elderly woman who makes the most amazing bread I've ever tasted! No matter what I said or how much I complimented her, she never divulged her secret ingredient. I visited with her every time I went to the market. The stall next to her sold books, and I took delight in rifling through and finding good cultural and historical reads. I have a collection of books from each country I've lived in."

"Your description makes me feel as though I am there!" Leah said. "The market sounds like quite an experience, and Madame Anais seems lovely. On a much smaller scale, there's a farmer's market here in town every weekend during the summer. The sellers offer mostly flowers or crafts and set up tables next to the local farm. Everything at the farm is organic, and they're open through three seasons. All the fruits, vegetables, and baked goods are exceptional. They even make their own jams and salad dressings, and they provide stock to Jenny's! Depending on the season, the farm offers hayrides to pick your own flowers, berries, or pumpkins.

We're fortunate to have this treasure in our little town. JJ and I frequently stop by, and we'd love for you to join us!"

"I definitely look forward to visiting the farm when they open for the season, and I'd be delighted to go with you and JJ."

"I think you would also appreciate our local library," Leah added. "It's a national historic landmark and has twice won the award for 'Best Small Library in America.' The architecture is incredibly detailed, with carved granite, decorative archways, and gargoyles on the building's highest points. Behind the library is a beautifully landscaped garden with brick walkways, a fountain, and a small stage with a pergola. JJ and I enjoy the garden, and of course the children's wing inside the library, but I'm sure you would like it in its entirety. In fact, the prominent family who lived here in the nineteenth century worked with the architects who designed and built several of the buildings in our Main Street area, including the library. There's such magnificent beauty and history here. When the weather warms, I can give you a walking tour, if you'd like."

"Absolutely! I didn't know, even having grown up nearby, that this quaint town boasted such an honored history. I am indeed intrigued."

"In addition, there are a few parks in town, aside from the one we visited with the playground and the baseball field. Each park has its own unique landscape and characteristic trails. My favorite is the historic rustic estate and grounds that were formerly occupied by a member of the same prominent family who resided in town. The trails around the property contain a small brook and open meadows. My favorite spot is the garden pond and the surrounding large oak trees. It's so calm and peaceful. I love the sound of the leaves rustling in the breeze and the ripple of the water as it reaches the flowers and lily pads."

"We must include the estate in our walking tour. Your words portray a beautiful image of its grounds."

Leah smiled. "You mentioned that there are many parks in Paris. Did you have a favorite?"

"Yes, there's one park in Paris that I frequently visited for a run or a walk. Parc Monceau, in the eighth arrondissement, features a historical section with statues of French poets and composers. That section, of course, was an interesting draw for me. The park also includes a spacious open garden, a fascinating variety of trees, and a pond with a small bridge. There are Renaissance structures throughout the park, and each season brings a new look and feel to the garden. It's quite stunning. The colorful landscape in autumn was a highlight for me, and the park was always a welcome green retreat when I needed a break from the bright lights of the city."

"Parc Monceau seems like my kind of place for sure!" She sat back in her chair and sighed dreamily.

"I'll remember that. Are you ready for dessert?"

"Yes, please!"

Eric retrieved the crème brulée for each of them and handed Leah the cream for her espresso. She offered the cream to him when she was finished with it, but he held up a hand. "Do you really drink it black?"

"Always."

"That must be so strong."

"It is, but I like the bold taste from the beans."

"You make me feel strong." She propped her chin on her hands, smiling at him with humor in her eyes.

"I see what you did there." He laughed along with her.

"It really was a brilliant thing to say to JJ, though. It still amazes me how well you can get through to him."

"Thank you," Eric said. "I really enjoy being with him, and he's making great progress. Speaking of which, I spoke to the high school principal earlier today, and she said we can bring JJ by anytime Sunday afternoon. The school will be open for a basketball game, so there will be some people inside, but it shouldn't be crowded, especially in the auditorium. Does that work for you?"

"I can't believe the winter concert is next weekend already! Thank you for setting up a rehearsal for him at the school," she replied. "Yes, we can meet you there. One o'clock? We were going to play with the puppies at Kay's Sunday afternoon. Would you want to join us after we practice at the school? She has a fenced area behind her place for the dogs to run unleashed."

"That sounds like a great plan." He paused. "Aside from dance, what would you wish you could do or be?"

"That's a good one. I always enjoyed creative writing in school, and I love kids, so maybe I'd wish to write children's stories. Though I'd definitely have to collaborate with an illustrator, because I can't draw at all! How about you, what would you wish?"

"I'd wish to be an athlete," he said. "I would like to think I'm good at sports, but I'm really not. It seems we both have an interest in writing, though I write research papers, not stories."

"Really? Have your papers been published?"

"Publishing has always been a goal, but one I've not yet achieved. I always attach a copy of my papers to my resume, but so far, no one has been interested. I'm required to complete specific reports on my research, and that's what management has always wanted. The papers I write include not only my thoughts, but also ideas for making advancements in the field, through the combination of music and other techniques I've found success with."

"Is it possible to send your papers out as is, instead of attached to a resume for a job position?"

"Typically, you need to be affiliated with the organization first before they'd entertain the possibility of reviewing any written work. Though, I suppose it couldn't hurt to try."

"I would think that Boston is a great place to investigate, with its renowned colleges and media forums."

"You're right, that's a great idea. I'll look into it. Thank you, I really appreciate it."

"I'm glad I could finally help you!"

He reached out and held both of her hands. "You've inspired me in other ways, Leah. In creating tonight for you, I made a matching donation to the local chapter of the Arc, to support children and adults with intellectual and developmental disabilities."

Leah's eyes brightened, and she brought his hands up to her cheek. "Yes, I'm familiar with the Arc. That's wonderful!"

"Other than the furniture, which are rentals, everything here is for you," Eric continued. "Please, tell me you'll accept it all."

"I will cherish everything, thank you!" She rested her head on his hands, then popped it back up when she realized. "The tapestry?"

"It's yours."

"But…it's magnificent!"

"That's exactly why I want you to have it. I want you to remember tonight and have hope for the future. It'll fit perfectly on the wall in your long hallway upstairs. I'll help you hang it."

"I will always remember tonight for so many reasons. Dinner was fabulous, by the way." Leah took in the dazzling image of the tapestry, closed her eyes, and pictured Eric and herself strolling, arm in arm, in that very spot. "I will have happy dreams every time I walk by my hallway. Thank you so much."

"I'm delighted." He tenderly caressed her hands.

"What's your biggest accomplishment?" she asked.

"That's easy, being able to help my family, and all the families I've had the pleasure to work with. You?"

"JJ, without a doubt. What's your biggest fear?"

"Hmm. Certainly, there are things that worry me or make me feel nervous, just like anyone else, but I wouldn't say that I have any really big fears. While I may not be interested, for example, in skydiving, I don't have a fear of heights, or of free falling. Not sure if that really answers your question. What about you?"

"I'm not a thrill seeker, and things like that do scare me, but my biggest fears are either something happening to JJ or something happening to me that would make me unable to take care of him."

"I can understand that. Let's hope that never happens. How about...your most embarrassing time?"

"The nineties!" Leah laughed. "I had long, crimped hair and wore big overalls. Of course, back then, I thought I looked great."

Eric joined in her merriment. "Yes, those baggy jeans and sweaters! I had long, straight hair over my ears, but I was very cool."

"I bet you were 'da bomb!'" Leah found great amusement in thinking back to her teenage years.

"I'm confident that you, my lovely lady, were 'lookin fly!'" Eric turned the music off, scrolling through his phone to find a nostalgic song. "One more dance?"

Leah went into his arms again, as Savage Garden's "Truly Madly Deeply" filled the room. "I loved this song!"

"Did you know that this song is about two lovers who had been separated, then found their way back to each other? In addition, the music video was filmed on the streets of Paris."

"Really? I knew it was a love song, but I didn't know the story, and I definitely didn't know the video was filmed in Paris. That's so interesting!"

He spun her as he had before, though he stopped her once her back was against him. There, they became immersed in the music and the lyrics, even after the song ended. With his head close to hers, Eric's cheek brushed her silky skin, as he whispered in her ear, "*Je tombe amoureux de toi*...I'm falling in love with you."

Leah turned toward him, gently stroked his beard, then rested her hands there as she caressed his lips with hers. "I'm falling in love with you too," she whispered in return.

This new year, she relished, *has already been beyond compare…and now, the new year holds an incomparable love.*

Eric wrapped his arms around her back, while she wrapped hers around his neck, and they ended the evening with a long, tender kiss.

Chapter Eleven

"I'm nervous, Mommy."

Leah glanced back at JJ through the rearview mirror. He began to fidget with his fingers and the tie-string of his pants while he stared out the window; this had happened many times before. He had been so excited when they had left their apartment, but now that the destination was near, his anxiety had kicked in.

JJ had been to the high school before to attend past winter concerts. He knew that they would park near the football field and that the auditorium would be to their right after they entered the school. He knew that the gym was located across from the auditorium and that a basketball game would be in progress. He also knew which classroom behind the stage would be open as the designated "quiet" room for Bridge of Music students who needed a break from the crowd and noise.

The annual recital and dress rehearsal for Leah's dance studio was always held at the high school, and sometimes JJ played on the stage or in the backstage area in between rehearsals or during intermission. Those were all routine for him. However, he had never been on the high school stage before as part of a performance. He knew that was the reason for their trip to the school that day, and the novelty changed everything, which presented challenges.

"It's okay to be nervous. I still get nervous before a performance and many of my dance students do too. That's why we have extra practices and rehearsals, especially on the stage, so we can get all our nervousness out and be ready for the performance." Leah tried to comfort him, hoping that if he knew he wasn't alone in his feelings, then he would be calmed. As she pulled into the parking lot of the school, she saw Eric leaning against his car. "Look, JJ, Eric's here, and we can park next to him."

Eric opened Leah's door and immediately noticed the concern in her eyes. Through silent communication, he nodded his head and massaged her hands, letting her know that he understood. He went over to the other side of the car and opened JJ's door.

"Hi, buddy!" he said, presenting a cheerful greeting to JJ.

"I'm nervous, Mr. Eric."

Eric leaned in and unbuckled JJ's seatbelt. "I'm a little bit nervous too, but we're going to do this together. Right now, I really need a hug from you." He stepped back and opened his arms.

JJ peeked out of the car in one direction, then the other. He saw a couple of older boys in the parking lot and waited for them to disappear into the school before he got out of the car. Then, he swiftly ran into Eric's arms, though he tucked his own arms against himself and kept his head down.

Eric held JJ tightly for a moment. "Thanks for the hug. I feel better already! First goal, JJ, is that we are going to walk to the door. Do you want your mom to come with us?"

JJ nodded. Eric kept an arm around JJ as they walked, and Leah stayed close to JJ's other side.

Once they reached the door, Eric bent down to meet JJ's eyes. "Today is for us to practice. I'm going to focus on you, and I want you to focus on me. We are not going to focus on what other people are doing. On the day of the concert, there will be more people inside, but they'll be focused on what they need to do. We are going to focus on our next goal, which is to walk inside and down the hallway to the quiet room." Eric stood and pulled JJ close to his side.

As Eric opened the door and entered the school, JJ buried his face in Eric's side, though he peeked out briefly at the people in the lobby. Once they made it to the quiet room, he waited for Eric to open the door, then cautiously looked inside. The room was empty, other than Eric's guitar. JJ ran over to where the guitar sat on a table.

Eric placed an arm around Leah's shoulders as they walked in together. "We're getting there." He smiled at her, and her eyes lightened.

"Mr. Eric, what's this?" JJ pointed to the black pole that stood near the guitar.

"That's the microphone stand, and this is the microphone." Eric pulled it out of the stand and handed it to JJ. "Right now, it's off, but when we go on stage, I'll plug it into the amplifier and turn it on. The sound of the guitar and our voices will be bigger, so that everyone in the audience can hear us. I want you to hear what that will sound like."

"Mommy, where are Aunt Kay and Stef?"

"They aren't here now because it's just a rehearsal. They will definitely be here waiting for you on the day of the concert, and they'll have your iPad."

"Where will you be, Mommy, when it's my turn?"

"I can stand in the wings, just off-stage, but so that you can see me."

Eric added, "And shortly before our turn, I'll come here to bring you to the stage. That's our next goal. We're going to pretend that someone else is performing on the stage, and we're going to walk to the wings to get ready for our turn. I'm going to send your mom to the wings now, ahead of us." He winked at Leah to let her know all would be okay, and she smiled in return.

"Love you, JJ!" Leah gave him a quick hug.

After Leah left, Eric threw the guitar over his shoulder, scooped up the folding chair and microphone stand in one arm, and wrapped his other arm around JJ. As they headed to the stage, Eric repeated, "Remember, focus only on me. You're doing a great job making me feel strong, JJ."

"No, amazing!" JJ corrected, his face again buried in Eric's side.

"Yes, buddy. Amazing!" As they approached the stage, Eric informed JJ, "Okay, listen. The rules for everyone in the stage area are no running and voices at a whisper until our turn. Got it?" He felt JJ nod his head.

They entered the stage area, and Eric brought JJ to a corner near the front wing, where Leah happened to be. "Mom's here, JJ," Eric whispered.

JJ quietly went over to Leah and hugged her. "It's dark in here."

"Yes, JJ." Eric acknowledged. "You told me that you didn't want the lights on. Once we go on stage, there will be a spotlight on us so that the audience can see us. It will be a very bright light, but you can look at me or your mom. If you don't like it, let me know, and we will turn the house lights on, okay?"

"Okay, Mr. Eric."

"Great. Now, on the day of the concert, we'll be waiting here for a little while, watching other people perform on stage. Let's pretend it's our turn now to go on stage. Let me set everything up, then I'll come get you, okay?"

"Okay, Mr. Eric." JJ held on tightly to Leah and watched as Eric set up the equipment.

"Here we go, buddy." Eric held out his arms and JJ snuggled in as they walked on stage. "I need your help now, JJ. Give my guitar a big squeeze until I sit down." Eric slid his guitar in between JJ and himself until JJ released his grip on him. Eric quickly sat down, placing a hand on JJ's shoulder while he put the guitar on his lap with the other. "Are you okay with the spotlight, or do you want the house lights on?"

JJ looked towards the spotlight and shaded his eyes. He could only see a few seats in the front, which made him happy, because he didn't want to be able to see the audience. When he looked into the wings, he clearly saw his mom. He rested his hands on Eric's shoulder. "I'm okay with the spotlight."

"Great. Here we go." Eric began to perform their song.

JJ covered his ears from the increase in volume, but he remained on stage next to Eric. Midway through the song, JJ uncovered his ears, though he didn't sing.

When Eric finished, he stood and put an arm around JJ. "Thank you for giving me the strength to perform the whole song. We did it! Should we practice the song one more time?"

"No, I know all the words."

"Okay, buddy." Eric walked JJ over to Leah, then went back for the equipment.

"We did it, Mommy!"

"I'm so proud of you!" Leah embraced him tightly, near tears. Her little boy had made it onto the stage. She had captured the moment through photos and a short video, which she sent to Eric's phone. *That was a huge success!* she thought.

"Before we go, JJ, is there anything that you want to practice again or any questions you have?" Eric asked as he put the equipment back in the corner of the wings; it belonged to the school. His guitar was already over his shoulder.

"No, I'm good. I want to go now."

"You were amazing, JJ!" Eric ruffled the boy's hair.

"You were amazing too, Mr. Eric, and it wasn't too loud."

"Oh, I'm pleased to hear that, JJ. Thank you!"

Leah embraced Eric. "You truly are amazing. Thank you so much!"

"My pleasure."

* * *

JJ ran up to the window, plastering his hands and nose on the glass. Kay and Stef waved to him, and the dogs on the grooming tables barked a greeting.

"They don't open every Sunday, but since they'll have to close next weekend because of the concert, they opened today," Leah informed Eric. "They own six female Shih Tzu puppies, three pure-breds and three rescues, all of varying ages. They're technically all adult dogs, but we call them puppies, because they're so cute!"

"I look forward to meeting them."

"Have you owned any pets?" Leah asked.

"We had a fish tank when Ben and I were kids, but that's it."

"We did too! Some of the fish would look at me through the glass when I'd talk to them…kind of like what JJ's doing now!" She laughed.

"That's adorable." He tucked her hair behind her ears.

Kay came around from behind the glass. "Hi! I just let the puppies out back."

"Yay!" JJ bolted past Kay, who had her arms open.

"What, no hug?" she called after JJ.

Leah took the offering. "I'll hug you!" She then whispered to Kay, "Thank you, and please thank Stef, too, for the other night."

Kay extended her arms so she could look at Leah. "And?"

"It was magical." Leah glowed with elation.

"Excellent." Kay then directed her attention to Eric, giving him a quick hug and pat on the back. "You're a good man."

"Thanks, Kay, and tell Stef I say hello."

"I'll tell her. Go play with the puppies."

The air was cool, but not bitterly so, and the ground was dry and free of snow. Jackets were a necessity, and their breath fogged the air, but the wind was calm, and the sun warmed the shadows. Leah and Eric watched all six dogs as they chased after JJ, who was full of laughter. When he quickly changed his direction, two of the dogs bumped into each other, then pawed and sniffed at one another.

"Puppies, Mommy!" JJ sped toward Leah and Eric.

Then, all six puppies dashed over to Leah, tails wagging excitedly and little legs pawing at hers. Before she had a chance to pet them, they surrounded Eric and sniffed with great interest. Leah took Eric's arm and guided him to sit on the ground with her, legs out straight. At that point, some of the puppies jumped over her legs, while the others jumped over Eric's. JJ kneeled on the ground near them and pulled up blades of grass.

Leah leaned forward and laughed as the puppies tried to lick her face. One curled up into a ball on her lap. She picked up and kissed a puppy with brown and white spots. "This is Poet-Yi. She is the oldest of the six and also the tiniest. And precious, aren't you?" Leah cooed at the puppy as she wagged her tail. Poet-Yi looked away from Leah to Eric, then to JJ. Leah laid her down on Eric's lap, and she curled up on him.

Another puppy, whose hair was a silky black, sniffed behind Eric curiously. Leah picked her up, but she wiggled out of Leah's grasp and laid her front paws on the ground with her tail up in the air. "This silly one is Liliana." Leah threw the squeaky ball that was next to her, and Liliana retrieved it, but brought it to JJ.

A small puppy, mostly white, with brown shading on her back and black on her ears and around her eyes, padded next to Leah and licked her hand. She petted the dog's head and scratched her ear. "This little one is Aria. She'll follow you around, and she loves snuggles!" Leah picked her up and put her on Eric's lap next to Poet-Yi.

The two puppies that played with each other and jumped over Leah's legs were similar in color pattern, white with some brownish and grayish patches. "I call those two 'the twins' because of their coloring, but they're different in size. The smaller one is Abby, and the bigger one is Kyara." They scampered over to JJ, who was playing fetch with Liliana.

Leah petted the black and white spotted puppy on her lap. "And this snuggly one is Mai-Li. She loves to be held, and her favorite toy is the chewy bone. She holds the toy between her paws. It's very cute!"

"They all seem very friendly and lovable." Eric continued to pet the two on his lap. "I don't think I can move now. I don't want to disturb them."

"My dad always said the same thing," Leah reminisced fondly. "Kay had Poet-Yi first, before my dad passed. He adored Poet-Yi, and was always on the floor playing with her."

Soon, the three lap dogs awoke and crawled off Leah and Eric. Then, they all joined JJ and the other dogs in games of fetch, tug-of-war, and chase. Laughter, barks, and a few howls punctuated the fun-filled atmosphere.

Eric spun JJ around, who shrieked with amusement, then he dropped to the ground with his arms extended out from his shoulders. JJ rolled over him to lie on the ground next to him. Eric reached up to grab Leah's hand and pulled her down by his other side.

All six puppies jumped from person to person and licked their faces. Leah and Eric exchanged a loving glance, as she reached over to brush the hair off his forehead. Then, JJ rolled between them, and they tickled him while he squirmed and giggled.

* * *

After a long but exhilarating day, Leah stretched her arms and was about to turn out her light when Eric called.

"Hi, Leah. Did I wake you?"

"I was just about to go to sleep."

"I wish I was there with you."

"Me too."

"I wanted to wish you good night, and to let you know that Madelyn had the baby tonight."

"Oh, that's so exciting!" Leah said. "How is she? What's the baby's name?"

"She's tired, but fine. Cameron James Hynes, healthy boy. I'll text you a picture."

"Congratulations, Uncle Eric!"

"Yeah, 'uncle' sounds really great, thanks! Ben is spending the night in the hospital. He asked if you and I could come see the baby in the morning. My parents and Mrs. Dalton plan on spending the afternoon there."

"I would love to see the baby in the morning!"

"Great. I'll pick you up at nine?"

"I'll be ready!"

"Sleep well, Leah."

"Goodnight, Eric."

After their call disconnected, Eric's text came through. The baby was swaddled in a hospital blanket, with a white knit cap on his head. He was peacefully asleep, his tiny fingers gripping the blanket. Eric captioned:

Cameron James, born January 29th, 7lbs 8oz, 20 inches long

* * *

Leah and Eric walked hand in hand into the bustling hospital lobby, and found the elevator that would stop at the maternity floor. Ben had given Eric Madelyn's room number, so it was a quick find. When they entered the room, they saw Madelyn nursing the baby, and Ben sitting by her bed, one hand on the baby's head, while his other stroked Madelyn's hair.

The tender scene caused Leah to stop for a moment. She turned away and stepped back into the hallway.

Eric noticed her hesitation and wrapped an arm around her. "Is something wrong?"

"Certain memories from when I gave birth just hit me hard," she replied. "I was in a very different place, emotionally, back then. I need to try to block out those unpleasant memories and think only of the good ones, like holding JJ for the first time." She took a deep breath. "I'll be fine. I want to be present for Ben, Madelyn, and Cameron. I just need a minute."

"I'm here for you." He held her gently for a few minutes, and she relaxed into him.

"I'm ready now."

He kept an arm around her as they walked into the room. Ben noticed them and with long strides went over to Eric for a brotherly embrace.

"Congrats, little bro."

"He's here, he's finally here. It's beyond words," Ben gushed.

"You're not going soft on me now, are you?" Eric teased, patting Ben's shoulder.

"No way." Ben deepened his voice and stood at attention. Then, he softened. "Okay, maybe a little. I bet you will too, big bro." Ben simulated a punch to Eric's chest. Then, he turned to Leah and hugged her. "I'm glad you could come. Madelyn will be happy to see you."

"Congratulations, Ben!"

Madelyn had finished the baby's feeding, and was now rocking him while he slept. Leah placed her gift bag on Madelyn's bed then gently hugged her. "Congratulations, mama!" She spoke softly, touching the baby's head. "He's precious. How are you feeling?"

"Thanks Leah," Madelyn replied. "I'm a little sore, a lot tired. One minute I'm on cloud nine, the next I'm crying, but he's an absolute wonder. I can't even explain it."

"I totally get it." Leah hugged Madelyn again. "Enjoy the journey. You're going to be a great mom."

"And now I'm crying again! Here, take him."

Leah laughed. "Gladly!" She moved the gift bag closer to Madelyn's reach and sanitized her hands. "This is for Cameron and you." Then, she carefully transferred the baby from Madelyn's arms to hers.

Cameron opened his mouth and a little bubble popped. Soft newborn noises came from him as he slept, and he snuggled his head toward Leah's chest. Tiny fingers stretched over the blanket, and when Leah massaged his palm with her finger, he gripped it tightly.

"Welcome to the world, Cameron. You are so sweet." She cooed to him, and kissed his velvety cheek. "Oh, the newborn baby powder smell and the snuggles. I miss this!" She rocked him and turned to face Eric. "This is your Uncle Eric, Cameron." She met Eric's eyes, which were light and close to tears. "Meet your nephew."

Eric placed a hand by the baby's head. "He's angelic." He walked over to Madelyn and bent to kiss her forehead. "Congratulations, Madelyn."

"Thank you." Madelyn squeezed Eric's hand with sisterly affection.

"Eric, you should hold your nephew," Leah suggested.

"Oh, I don't know. I love kids, but the small babies make me nervous. Once he's able to run around, I'll happily hold him."

"Are you afraid?" Leah challenged him.

"No, not afraid. Just a little nervous. I don't want to hurt him."

"I'll help you." Leah shifted the baby up her arm so she could fully support him on one side. With her free hand, she took Eric's and led him to a chair. She gave him a squirt of hand sanitizer and gestured for him to sit. Then, she grabbed the nursing pillow and placed it over Eric's lap. "Round your arms in front of you and rest them on the pillow," she instructed. Once he did so, she carefully placed the baby in his arms on the pillow. She lifted Eric's elbow so that the baby's head was supported by his arm. "You just need to support his head, because he can't yet support it himself." She bent down in front of him and placed his hands on Cameron's belly. "Now, just breathe him in. He can sense your emotions. What do you think?"

As he stared at the tiny being in his arms that yawned, making a perfectly round "O" with his mouth, Eric smiled, and a tear of joy fell onto his cheek. "It's sublime." Warmth and tenderness shone in his eyes as he looked at Leah. "Thank you."

Leah wiped the tear away and brushed her lips over his cheek. "You're welcome. Enjoy him."

Ben placed a hand on Eric's shoulder. "What did I tell you?"

"Yeah." Eric touched the baby's cheek, and his tiny fingers stretched. "Yeah, you're right, Ben."

Leah snapped a picture of the brothers with the baby and shared it to Eric's and Madelyn's phones.

"Leah, these are adorable!" Madelyn took out the baby sleepers from the gift bag. "And all different sizes, that's great! A rattle and teether, so cute, and diapers, very grateful for those! Oh my goodness, a silk sleep mask! Thank you so, so much!"

"You're very welcome! I'm glad you like everything," Leah said. "Enjoy the sleep mask, especially when you can only grab moments here and there to rest. It's very calming. I still use mine."

"Very generous of you, Leah. Thank you." Ben hugged her.

"Leah, would you please give them my gift? I put it on the counter over there," Eric asked, while he continued to hold the baby.

Madelyn opened Eric's gift and unfolded a large blue blanket with teddy bears on it. "Oh, Eric, it's beautiful, thank you!" Madelyn had a brief flashback as she looked at the blanket. "Ben, didn't you have a blanket similar to this?"

Ben held the blanket. "It does look familiar."

"It was yours, Ben," Eric informed them.

"It was mine?"

"Yeah. When I was helping mom and dad clean out the house for their move a couple of years ago, I found the blanket. I knew that the day would come when you would need it, so I had it professionally cleaned and repaired. The edges were all frayed, and there were a couple of tears in the fabric, along with several stains. I've been holding onto it for you. You used to drag that blanket around with you everywhere, and you sucked your thumb. I used to call you 'Linus.' Do you remember?"

Ben held the blanket out in front of him, and the memories came back. "Looking more closely, I can see where some of the repairs were made, but it looks almost new. I remember now, yeah, I loved this blanket. When I started first grade, mom told me that it needed to go to blanket heaven, but it would be watching over me. I was devastated, but then she gave me a baseball and all was good again." Ben handed the blanket to Madelyn and went over to his brother. "Thank you, Eric."

"You've always been our biggest cheerleader, Eric. Thank you so much for everything," Madelyn expressed with heartfelt gratitude.

"You're my family." Eric looked down at the baby. "My family." Then, the baby scrunched his face and began to cry. "Whoa, it's okay. Don't cry."

Leah scooped the baby into her arms and shushed him, walking around the room with him. Once he quieted, she handed him back to Madelyn. "Back to mama, sweet Cameron." She went to Eric and wrapped an arm around him, looking at him endearingly. After the devotion she had just witnessed between Eric and his family, the glimmer inside her grew significantly brighter.

Chapter Twelve

The final week before the winter concert was always very busy for Leah: extra rehearsals for her dance team, coordinating efforts with the high school, a trip to the printer's for Dance World brochures and business cards.

This year, Leah also had the added layer of JJ's performance. A successful experience for JJ would build his self-confidence so that he could learn and grow. However, a failed experience could cause JJ to develop a fear of singing, or the stage, or the high school, or any other possible trigger connected to the concert. Before he could gain the emotional capacity to learn from failure, JJ would have an uphill battle to overcome his fear, first. Because of that, Leah tried to keep each day as calm and as positive as possible, for his benefit.

"So, today was your last practice with Eric before the concert in just a few days."

"I know, Mommy."

"How are you feeling about it?"

"Amazing! I know all the words and so does Mr. Eric. I can go on the stage and help him."

"I'm so happy to hear that!" she said. "Get a good night's sleep. Love you!"

"I love you, Mommy."

Leah turned out his light and closed his bedroom door. Before she went into her room, she looked one more time at the tapestry hung on the wall in the hallway. She ran her hand along the glittering lights of the Eiffel Tower and took in a blissful breath as she recalled that magical evening.

Eric was busy with final preparations for the concert on his end, as well. Even so, he had made time each day for Leah, either with a quick lunch together, or with a phone call of sweet wishes at the end of the day before sleep.

As she retired for the night, her phone chimed. "Hi! I was just thinking about you," she said, sending her affectionate greeting through the line.

"Well, I'm definitely pleased to hear that. You're always on my mind."

"Before I came to bed, I was looking at my magnificent tapestry, and remembering our magical time together."

"That's exactly why I wanted it on your wall."

"Dream of me, tonight?"

"My lovely lady, I dream of you every night."

As Leah drifted off to sleep, her inner joy expressed itself on her peaceful face, while she dreamed of him.

* * *

The days became lively in the house once Ben and Madelyn had returned home with the baby. Since Eric's parents had arrived earlier than planned, they had found a room at a nearby inn and decided to stay there for the remainder of their visit. They had also very generously covered a room for Mrs. Dalton, so she could enjoy some privacy as well. With gratitude, Eric continued his sojourn in the guest room, rather than in the basement.

On that morning, all was quiet in the kitchen, for the time being, anyway. Eric started the brew for the coffee pot. Mrs. Dalton had already arrived and was in the bathroom with Madelyn for Cameron's first bath. Eric's parents were anticipated to be by later that morning. Ben was outside with his truck and a container of engine oil.

Eric took advantage of the momentary silence to enjoy a cup of coffee before a hectic day of work. He had offered his assistance to the lighting and sound crews for the high school; final set-up for the concert was happening that morning, followed by his final lessons with his students that afternoon, in addition to his regular therapy sessions. Eric was not scheduled to work with JJ, but he believed that JJ was ready.

After a few meditative breaths, Eric felt ready for his day. While he rinsed his coffee cup, an unfamiliar number buzzed through on his phone. He made himself available to all the parents of his students and clients, though he hadn't set up everyone's information in his contacts. He answered the call only because he assumed it was one of the parents.

"Hello?" he began. "Yes, this is Eric Hynes... Oh, good day, sir, how are you?" He turned to lean his back against the sink. "That's good to hear. I'm doing fine, thank you...Yes, that's correct, I did...Oh, well, I appreciate your calling to let me know... You don't say..." He stood up straight with a hand on his hip. "You have my sincere gratitude, sir. Yes, I am definitely interested...Excuse me?" He sat back down at the table. "When, sir?... I understand... Yes, thank you... Same to you, sir."

Eric placed his phone on the table, rested his head in his hands, and closed his eyes.

"She's back up and running! Thankfully, all she needed was the oil change." Ben breezed in and washed the oil from his hands at the kitchen sink. He noticed Eric's weary countenance. "Hey, bro, is the baby keeping you up at night?" When Eric didn't reply, Ben sat down next to him and tapped his back. "Eric?"

"Oh, hey, Ben." Eric let his hands fall from his head onto the table, but remained hunched over with his head down.

"Are you not getting enough sleep because of the baby crying at night?"

"Oh, no, I'm not tired. The baby crying isn't a problem."

"Then...what is the problem?"

Eric looked at his brother. "University of Copenhagen just called. They've offered to publish my research papers."

"That's fantastic! I know you've been wanting that to happen for a long time now. So, why aren't you celebrating?"

"They'll only publish my papers if I accept a position with them."

"Okay, what's the position?"

"They want me to head their research department," Eric said. "They're interested in learning about the therapeutic strategies that I've had success with and how they could incorporate my findings into their standards. They've also offered to publish any future papers I write regarding the research I would be doing for them. This is probably the most prestigious opportunity I have ever been offered and it could mean making advancements in the field and, ultimately, improving resources for supporting families."

"That's great, Eric. Will you be able to work remotely from here?"

"No. I..." Eric paused when Madelyn came in.

"Hi, guys! Cameron was not a fan of bathing. Mom is getting him dressed now, and I need to warm up some milk that I pumped. Then, he should be a much happier baby."

Ben laid a comforting hand on Eric's shoulder, then went over to Madelyn and kissed her cheek. "Can I do anything for you?"

"Thank you, but I'm all set with Mom for right now." With a concerned look in her eyes, she tilted her head toward Eric, but Ben gestured for her not to worry.

"Eric, I need your help with some cables for the truck. Can you come with me, please?"

Eric nodded and followed his brother outside. He leaned his back against the truck, crossed his arms over his chest, and rolled his sneakered foot over the stone driveway.

Ben had never seen Eric so distressed. His older brother had always been his rock, and he would do whatever he could to help him before the rock crumbled. "So, why can't you work remotely?"

"I'd have to work directly with the other speech pathologists, along with physicians and scientists. I would have to move to Copenhagen. They've offered to cover my flight out there, as well as to set me up with temporary housing."

"When would you need to go?"

"Sunday afternoon."

"What about Leah?"

With a pained expression, Eric looked at Ben. "I don't know," he replied. "All I know is that I can't talk to her about this right now. Tomorrow is the concert, and there's too much riding on it for JJ. I can't hinder that for her, or for him. There has to be a way to make this work, though. Love always finds a way, right?"

Ben pulled his brother in for an embrace. "I have to be honest with you. From what I've learned about Leah, I don't think a long-distance relationship would work for her. I have all the respect in the world for those who have successful long-distance relationships, but it's not for everyone and no one should be faulted for that. Let me ask you this, Eric: do you really want this position?"

Eric broke away from Ben's embrace. "Ben, you know that this is what I've wanted and worked hard to achieve for a long time."

"I've always admired your strong dedication to your work. Publishing your papers is what you've wanted...but do you really want a permanent position in research? You've always said that your passion is working with the kids."

"This position will have a positive impact on the kids' future. That's the driving factor for me."

"But will it make you happy—*truly* happy—here." Ben grabbed his brother's hand and placed it over Eric's heart. "For me, if I had to live in another country an ocean away from Madelyn and Cameron, I would not be happy, no matter how good the job was. You'll have to talk to Leah. Think about it, Eric. You know that we will support you, whatever you decide." Ben tapped Eric's shoulder, then left his brother alone to contemplate.

* * *

"Nice job, everyone! Again, from the top, facing away from the mirrors this time, and let me see those shining smiles!"

Leah started the music from the beginning and watched her dancers from behind. Their spacing was perfect, so she walked along the outer edge of the room for a view of them from the side. Lines were straight, transitions seamless. Then, she moved to the back wall where they faced forward. Individually, all the dancers smiled, pointed their feet, and extended their legs. As a group, they danced as one, powerfully emotional, with energy that flowed past their fingertips, out from their toes, and reached the far corners of the studio.

That was what she always taught all of her dancers, to feel the music, to feel the dance beyond just the choreography. Passion, love, and inspiration sparked when music and dance came together. Often, her dancers giggled at her when she spoke of dance in that manner, but their performance was evidence that they listened to her and understood her imagery.

Leah became misty-eyed and cupped her hands over her heart as they finished the dance, holding their final pose. "Yes, that's it! That was beautiful, exactly the way it needs to be performed tomorrow at the concert! Thank you all!"

"We like when we can make you cry, Ms. Leah!" one of the dancers piped up, as they all relaxed and sat on the floor.

"Happy tears!" Leah's smile gleamed, and she wiped her eyes with the backs of her fingers.

"We know, Ms. Leah. We want to make you proud!" another dancer called out.

"You *all* make me so proud!"

"Ms. Leah, don't dismiss us yet," Zelia declared, as she jumped up and ran toward the waiting area. The other dancers followed her, congregating by the door. Then, they all formed a close circle around Leah, and Zelia presented her with a bouquet of flowers. "We know how busy you'll be tomorrow, so we wanted to give this to you now."

"Thank you, Ms. Leah!" all the dancers chorused.

"You're all going to make me cry again! I love each and every one of you." Leah opened her arms, and they all crowded in for a group hug.

Through giggles, they all returned the sentiment. "We love you too, Ms. Leah!"

* * *

The night before a show still brought jittery excitement, even after all her seasoned years. Leah knew her team was ready, and she had everything she needed already prepared. Yet still, she couldn't settle her mind. JJ seemed eager for the concert, and she endeavored to keep her worries at bay. As an added precaution, she sent a hopeful wish into the universe for a smooth and successful performance for JJ.

She hadn't heard from Eric that day, so she gave him a call.

"There she is! I'm glad you called."

"I couldn't sleep, and I wanted to hear your voice."

"I'm always a phone call away, no matter what. No matter where I am. You know that, right?"

"Yes," Leah replied, though Eric's tone carried a hint of something unlike his usual charming demeanor. Maybe he was just tired. "Did you have a busy day?"

"Yeah, it was an uncommonly full day. I spent the morning at the high school helping with set up, along with my sessions at Bridge of Music in the afternoon."

"Are you ready for tomorrow?"

"I am. How about you?"

"My dancers are definitely ready. JJ appears to be ready. I just can't seem to unwind myself."

"*Laisser dormir*…let sleep in. I'll be there for you and JJ to-morrow."

He always knew exactly what to say, Leah thought, closing her eyes and letting out a breath. "I feel better now. Goodnight, Eric."

"Sleep well Leah."

She then fell into a restful slumber, though he managed only a few hours of fitful sleep.

Chapter Thirteen

For any novel or large event, Leah always made an early entrance with JJ. He was more likely to transition into the event successfully if he were among the initial few people who arrived. He usually asked if they could be the first ones to show up, though that wasn't always feasible, especially for the winter concert. There would be multiple vendors and other performer groups who would be arriving at the high school early for set up, prior to when the doors would open to the general public. Leah's dance team would be among those there in advance, and she had coordinated with Carolyn, who would stay with the dancers until she was able to get there. Classrooms behind the stage would be open, and each performer group was assigned to a specific classroom.

While still home, they were already behind schedule.

Clothing was one of JJ's triggers, due to his tactile sensitivities. He didn't like anything that touched his neck and often pulled at his shirts. Button-down collared dress shirts were always a struggle for him. Leah often bought a size larger than he needed, in order for the shirt to be looser around his neck.

JJ wanted the collar to be open wide and for several buttons to be unclasped. Leah allowed him to go without a tie, but the buttons needed to be fastened, other than the top one. Each time she got him calm enough to button the shirt, he put his hand under the collar and scratched his neck, then pulled away from her and unbuttoned the shirt again. After a lot of lotion on his neck, he finally accepted for the shirt to be reaffixed. Next was the dress pants and shoes, which presented similar challenges.

Because the dressing process took longer than usual, they got into the car later than she had hoped, and JJ's anxiety was already heightened before they even left their apartment. Though Leah always tried her best to keep her own stress level under control, she knew that JJ was sensitive to her emotions. He likely felt her anxiety compounded with his own.

She spoke as calmly and as confidently as she could muster. "Aunt Kay texted me, JJ. She and Stef are already in the quiet room waiting for you. Eric texted me, too. He's there helping the high school jazz band set up, but he'll come to see you once we get there. Other people are at the school setting up their stations, but we should still be able to arrive before the big crowd. We'll go directly to Aunt Kay and not focus on anyone else. We will be safe, and I'll hold onto you, okay?"

JJ didn't respond, but just stared out the car window. Leah gave him the iPad and hoped that would calm him. In addition, she needed a few deep breaths before she was ready to drive.

JJ was quiet during the ride and played with the iPad, until Leah pulled into the high school. He saw all the cars that were already parked, and several people walking in and out of the school, carrying various equipment and supplies. "I don't want to go in, Mommy."

She parked the car and turned to face him. "I'm here with you. We will do this together."

"No, I can't." He stiffened, and the iPad fell to the car's floor. Leah reached for the iPad and put it in her bag. She quickly went into the backseat with JJ, wrapping her arms around him for a tight hug; this was often a calming strategy for him. However, JJ pushed her away, flailing his arms and kicking his legs. She slid away from him to avoid contact with his limbs. Then, he screamed, eyes wide with fear.

"I want to go home! I don't want to go inside! I can't do it! I just want to go home!"

When JJ reached that state, Leah knew that all she could do was stay with him so that he wouldn't hurt himself. She had tried so many different strategies in the past, but found that she would have to either wait it out in the car until he self-calmed, or go home. Neither option would work for her, however, because she was also responsible for her dance team. She frantically texted Eric:

HELP! MELTDOWN IN THE CAR. BY THE FOOT-BALL FIELD.

Eric was in a conversation with the band directors when Leah's SOS came through. "Excuse me, please, I need to check on a student. Pleasure to meet you both." He quickly shook their hands, then strode through the auditorium and out of the building. He ran through the parking lot until he found Leah's car. As he threw open the back door, he pulled her up into his arms for a momentary embrace, wiped away her tears, then slid into the backseat.

JJ continued to display emotional dysregulation and didn't realize that Eric was there.

As Eric dodged JJ's flailing limbs, he unbuckled the seat belt and pulled JJ onto his lap. He leaned JJ's back against him, captured both of JJ's arms, crossed them, and brought them down to his lap, wrapping his own arms around JJ to apply deep pressure therapy. In addition, he was able to maneuver both of JJ's legs in between his own, though he was kicked in the process, and he applied gentle pressure to JJ's legs as well. Eric became a human weighted blanket around JJ.

Initially, JJ screamed louder and tried to break free, but with Eric's persistent, gentle pressure and body warmth, he gradually quieted and calmed. Then, JJ leaned his head on Eric's chest and closed his eyes.

Eric held JJ tightly for another minute, then relaxed the pressure. He moved JJ off his lap and sat him upright next to himself, brushing the young boy's hair off of his forehead.

JJ opened his eyes and saw Eric. "Hi, Mr. Eric."

"Hi, buddy." He smiled down at the innocent expression on JJ's face.

"Where's Mommy?"

"She's just outside the car. Let's get out of the car and say hi to her." Eric gently slid JJ over to the door and helped him out of the car.

Leah quickly wiped her tears away so that JJ wouldn't notice them. "Hi sweet face."

"Hi Mommy." He went into her arms. "I'm tired."

"Then let's go directly to Aunt Kay. It'll be quiet and calm in the room, and you can snuggle with her and Stef. I have your iPad, too."

"I need you and Mr. Eric to come with me. I don't want anyone to see me."

Leah looked at Eric, who smiled back at her while he nestled JJ in between them. They walked as one unit to the front of the school, and as Eric opened the door, JJ hid his face in Leah's shoulder. They continued together until they were in the quiet room. When they reached where Kay and Stef sat, Leah pulled JJ into an embrace.

"I'm so proud of you, JJ. I love you very much."

"I love you too, Mommy."

"Here are Aunt Kay and Stef."

JJ turned to them and requested, "Can we snuggle?"

"Absolutely!" Kay responded.

"Of course!" Stef said at the same time as Kay. She picked up a chair and put it between herself and Kay.

JJ hopped on to the chair, then laid his head on Kay's lap and extended his legs over Stef's.

On the table in front of them, Leah placed the iPad, along with JJ's water bottle and a bag of snacks.

"JJ, you did an amazing job walking to the quiet room. I'll come get you when it gets closer to our turn." Eric placed a comforting hand on JJ's shoulder.

"Okay, Mr. Eric. Bye, Mommy."

"Bye, sweet face." She blew kisses to Kay and Stef, then wrapped an arm around Eric as they walked out.

As soon as they were in the hallway, Leah faced Eric and held him close. "Thank you so much. He needed you."

"Leah, you kept him safe in the car, then got him in the building and down to the quiet room. JJ was very brave. We worked together."

She held him for a little while longer. Then, she wiped her eyes and collected herself. "I can't believe we made it in before the doors opened. I need to go check on my dancers, and I usually like to be in the lobby to greet people before the concert begins. Will I see you out there, or in the wings, maybe?"

"You will definitely see me."

Leah stopped in the bathroom first to fix her face and hair. As she looked at herself in the mirror, she smiled confidently and believed that all would be okay. JJ was inside and calm. "Let's go have a concert!" she said to her reflection.

After she had a motivational cheer with her dancers, Leah bundled her brochures and business cards into a small bag, then headed to the lobby. The doors had just opened, and the lobby was quickly filling with enthusiastic concertgoers.

A crowd had gathered in the lobby by the time Eric walked in. He looked around, then spotted Leah as she spoke to a few people. Suddenly, time stood still around her. Earlier, she had worn a coat, but now, her elegant lure enraptured him, once he saw what had been underneath it. She was radiant, shining in a full-length black dress with hints of gold sparkling throughout. The silky fabric hugged her arms and contoured her figure, with a soft flow around her ankles when she moved. The neckline of the dress was scooped, and she wore a delicate gold chain around her neck. Leah's hair was pulled over to one side, long as it caressed her shoulder, with a golden barrette on the other side. As she turned her head, her gaze found his, and she smiled her sideways smile meant only for him with a flutter in her lashes and a wave of her fingers. Her eyes shone as gold and bright as her dress. Eric melted and believed that he would become a puddle right there in the middle of the floor.

Somehow, he managed to deliver himself to her side, and he slipped his hand around her elbow.

"Eric, I would like you to meet Mrs. Callahan, principal of the high school, Mr. Costa, principal of the middle school, and Ms. Fontana, choral director of both schools." She turned her attention to those she had introduced. "This is Eric Hynes, speech and language pathologist and music instructor at Bridge of Music."

"Pleasure to meet everyone. Mrs. Callahan, we spoke a week ago. Thank you again for allowing JJ and me to rehearse last week."

"You're very welcome," she replied. "Nice to meet you as well, Mr. Hynes."

Eric shook their hands, then tightened his grip on Leah's elbow. "Would you excuse us, please?" Then he pulled her around the corner into a hallway that was separated from the crowd.

"What's wrong? Is it JJ?"

"JJ is perfectly fine." He faced her and held her hands. "You are stunning." As Leah's expression relaxed and her smile returned, he slowly ran his hands up her arms, then down again, immersing himself in the soft fabric under his fingers.

She stepped closer to him, letting her palms dance across his chest and under the collar of his shirt. The dark gray of his suit and tie over the blue of his shirt evoked the hues of the ocean as it flowed into the sea, just like his expressive eyes. "And you are very handsome, Mr. Hynes."

Eric enfolded her in his arms and closed his eyes. They were startled when a group of students came into the hallway with musical instruments.

Leah laughed softly. "Let's go. The concert is about to start."

The first half of the concert showcased the jazz bands, orchestras, and choral groups from the high school and middle school. Rows at the back of the auditorium were reserved for all performer groups. Leah usually sat with JJ for that half of the concert because he enjoyed the music. When she checked on him, he decided that he wanted to stay in the quiet room with Kay and Stef. Under the circumstances, she was fine with that and went into the auditorium to join her dance team. Across the way, she saw Eric sitting with Lydia and their students. He was positioned between a young boy on one side of him, and Angie was on his other side in her wheelchair, which was in the aisle near the ramp. He joked and laughed with the kids, who giggled right back at him. His caring manner with the children warmed her heart.

The jazz bands and orchestras were well-received by the audience. During the few minutes that the stage crew broke down the chairs and microphone stands, Leah strolled through the lobby, passing out Dance World brochures and speaking with vendors. Once the choral groups began, she went back to her dancers, and they quietly filed out of the auditorium. They would perform next.

In the wings, Leah and her dancers huddled in a circle and went through their pre-performance ritual. "Big smiles, big energy, feel the music, feel the dance!" Leah whispered. "All hands in. I love you all!" As a group, they whispered, "Dance World!" Then, they shimmied their hands up and over their heads.

Eric stood at the back of the wings, and watched Leah with her dancers. She glowed when she was with them, and they looked at her with pure adoration. Once the stage went black and the dancers ran on, he went up to her and brushed her hair off her shoulder.

"Oh! I didn't see you come in. You should watch them from the audience. It would look better that way."

The stage lights came on and the music began. Then, the dance came to life. "It looks perfect from here." Eric gazed at her while she watched her dancers with pride. Then, he became enthralled with the beauty of the story unfolding on the stage.

During the performance, the audience was silent, until the music and movement ended. At that point, they showed their appreciation with a standing ovation.

Eric stepped out of the way as the dancers ran off the stage toward Leah, practically knocking her over with their excitement.

"Beautiful! I'm so proud of all of you!" she congratulated her team.

Eric applauded. "Bravo, that was phenomenal!" The dancers giggled then, went back to their classroom. "Truly, that was awe-inspiring. You created that masterpiece."

"Thank you! This one in particular does mean a lot to me."

"The karate studio is setting up to go next, then the Bridge of Music students will go on, with JJ closing the show. We should go get him now."

With the iPad in his hands, JJ sat cross legged in the chair, playing happily, while Kay and Stef watched. The snack bag was just about empty.

"How are things going?"

JJ looked up at her. "Hi, Mommy. I'm building."

"It's all these different creatures that throw, drop, or sling a variety of shapes," Kay said, trying to explain the game.

"And somehow, he's able to use those shapes to build platforms with multiple levels," Steff added.

"It's fascinating to watch him," Kay commented.

"Yep, fascinating," Stef agreed.

"They're funny!" JJ said, while he continued to build on the game.

"He's been fine, by the way," Kay assured Leah.

"I'm very glad to hear that! Thank you both." Leah hugged each of them. "JJ, are you almost finished building that level?"

"Almost done, Mommy."

"Okay, but once you finish that level, you'll be all done with the iPad."

After a brief time, JJ put the iPad on his lap. "Can I do one more, Mommy?"

With a quick hand, Leah snatched the iPad and placed it in her bag. "Not now, JJ, but you can have it back once we are in the car."

Eric had pulled up a chair while he waited. "JJ, come over to me, please. I need to talk to you."

JJ ran over to Eric. "What is it, Mr. Eric?"

"First, high five or a hug?"

"Hug!" Enthusiastically, JJ hugged Eric.

While he held JJ in an embrace, Eric prepared him for the transition to the stage. "It's almost our turn, JJ. Right now, Ms. Lydia and your friends from Bridge of Music are all backstage in the wings for their performances. We are last, after Angie. I need your help, now, to get us to the wings."

"I don't want to go on the stage, Mr. Eric."

"That's okay. We don't have to if you don't want to. It would be very kind of you to cheer on your friends. They've worked so hard, and I want to cheer them on too. Can you help me?"

JJ straightened and looked at Eric. "Can Mommy come too?"

"Definitely!"

"Okay, I will help you cheer on our friends."

"Great! Thanks buddy!"

"Bye, Aunt Kay! Bye, Stef! Let's go, Mommy!"

"Bye, JJ!" Kay and Stef said in unison. Then, Kay whispered to Leah, "We'll be in the audience."

After one last hug to Kay and Stef, Leah joined JJ and Eric, who already had an arm around the boy. JJ buried his face in Eric's side during the short walk from the quiet room to the wings of the stage.

"JJ, Ms. Lydia and our friends are here." Eric walked JJ over to the group.

"Hello, JJ," Lydia greeted.

JJ kept his face buried against Eric's side, but he could hear the music on the stage. He peeked out with one eye, and saw a girl on the stage playing the flute. The stage lights and the house lights were on. One of the therapists from Bridge of Music was on the stage behind the girl. When the girl finished her song, the audience clapped, and the therapist told her to take a bow, then they walked off the stage. The girl received high fives from Ms. Lydia and the others in the group, including from Leah and Eric. However, JJ again hid his face and held onto his grip around Eric.

Next on stage was a boy who played a beginner drum pad and bell set. A different therapist went on stage to help the boy set up his instruments. Once the boy began to play, JJ released his grip on Eric and stepped in front of him to get a better view of the boy on the stage. Eric placed his hands on JJ's shoulders and smiled at Leah, who stood next to them.

"Mr. Eric, how many more kids are left?"

Eric whispered to JJ, "Two more, then Angie, then us."

"I still don't want to go on the stage."

"That's okay. Enjoy watching your friends."

Eric had spoken with the stage manager regarding JJ. Through headsets, the stage manager was in constant contact with the lighting and sound directors. If JJ would not perform, then Eric would signal the stage manager, who would close the curtain after Angie.

When the boy completed his percussion routine and came off the stage, another round of high fives ensued. That time, JJ also participated and gave a high five to the boy. Then, JJ looked back at his mom and Eric with a pleased expression on his face.

After two more performers, Angie independently rolled herself in her wheelchair onto the stage. Eric began to applaud, and the audience soon followed. She rolled one of the wheels of the wheelchair so that it spun her around. Then, her music began, and she sang a Taylor Swift song.

"We're next, JJ," Eric whispered.

"No, Mr. Eric."

"Are you sure you don't want to?"

"I don't want to."

"Okay." Eric signaled the stage manager with a thumbs down. The curtain would close when Angie was done.

As he watched Angie, JJ noticed that she looked very happy while she sang. When she finished her song, she clapped for herself and laughed. When the audience cheered for her, she spun herself around again in her wheelchair. JJ also liked to have fun, just like Angie did.

JJ turned to face Eric. "I'm ready to go on stage now, Mr. Eric."

"Are you sure, JJ?"

"Yes. I want to have fun like Angie, but I don't want the lights on."

"That's amazing, buddy! Stay here with your mom." Eric quickly went over to the stage manager, who was just about to close the curtain as Angie rolled herself off the stage. While the stage manager communicated with the lighting and sound directors, Eric grabbed his guitar, along with the microphone stand, amplifier, and chair that he had stored in a corner of the wings.

The audience and the stage went black while Eric set up the equipment on the stage. When he came back into the wings, the spotlight turned on.

"Okay, buddy. Here we go." Eric opened his arms, and JJ went from Leah's arms to Eric's.

Leah was already misty-eyed. She was joyfully astonished with JJ's last-minute change of heart. Eric winked at her as he brought her little boy onto the stage.

"Okay, buddy, I need your help. Give my guitar a big squeeze until I sit down." Eric did as they had rehearsed.

Then, JJ shaded his eyes and looked at the audience. He could see faces in the front, so he quickly looked into the wings and saw his mom. He also saw Ms. Lydia, Angie, and the other kids. When Eric began their song, JJ blocked his ears, but he looked at Eric.

After the first musical phrase of "You've Got a Friend In Me," JJ moved his hands to Eric's shoulder. Within the first verse, JJ began to hum along. When Eric heard JJ's hum, he looked at JJ and decided that he would sing to JJ, rather than to the audience.

By the second verse, JJ sang the lyrics along with Eric. JJ and Eric kept their eyes on each other and harmonized the remainder of the song together.

When they completed their song, the audience roared with applause, rising to their feet. JJ blocked his ears, dropping his head onto Eric's shoulder.

Eric stood and pulled JJ into his side. He lifted his guitar in the air with pride, then placed it on the stage. When he looked into the wings, he noticed tears running down Leah's face. He smiled at her, while he tapped his heart. The audience continued to cheer, so he held a hand over his heart and bowed his head, then presented his hand to JJ, which brought louder applause from the audience.

Eric bent down close to JJ's ears. "You're amazing, JJ!" When JJ peeked up at him, he prompted, "Help me take a bow, JJ. Like this."

With his eyes holding JJ's, he placed a hand over his heart. When JJ copied him, he bowed his head. JJ bowed his head, then Eric pulled JJ into an embrace. "Thank you for helping me, JJ. I'm proud of you!" Then, Eric brought JJ off the stage and the curtain closed.

"We did it, Mommy! It's amazing!" JJ ran into Leah's arms and, at the same time, he jumped up and down with excitement.

"I am so…so…proud of you! I love…you…very much!" Tears streamed down Leah's face, emotions overflowing from her heart, so much so that her voice became lodged in her throat.

"Are you crying happy tears, Mommy?"

The words would not come. All she could do was smile and nod her head as she cupped his face in her hands.

"I want high fives!" JJ went over to Ms. Lydia and the other the kids, who matched his fervor with congratulatory high fives.

From behind, Eric's arms enveloped Leah and he nuzzled her neck. She tilted her head so that it brushed against his, then he dried her cheeks with the touch of his hand.

"I have no words. 'Thank you' and 'you're amazing' don't even begin to express my gratitude, or how I feel about you and all that you've done for my son." She faced him and brushed his hair off his forehead, caressing his beard.

He took her hands in his and stroked her palms. "I can see it in your eyes and feel it from your heart. I feel the same for you and JJ. I hope you know that."

She wrapped her arms around him, rested her head on his chest, and he held her tighter still.

"All the kids are leaving now, Mommy. Can we go now?"

While in Eric's embrace, Leah looked toward her son. "Okay JJ. We just need to say goodbye to a few people." She stepped out of the embrace, but held onto one of Eric's hands. "Can you say good-bye and thank you to Eric?"

"Bye and thank you, Mr. Eric!" He hugged Eric tightly, while Eric rubbed his back and ruffled his hair.

"Bye, JJ." Eric had to clear his throat in order to hold back the tears welling in his eyes.

Then, JJ grabbed Leah's other hand and pulled her out of the stage area. She looked back at Eric and smiled. Their hands slipped apart until the tips of their fingers were no longer within reach.

Silence encased Eric, alone in the wings of the stage, as he ran a hand through his hair and a tear fell onto his cheek.

* * *

The quiet room was not so quiet when Leah and JJ walked in to collect their belongings. Family and friends gathered and cheered.

"Yay! Amazing!" JJ clapped along with everyone.

Leah thought she would tear up again as she thanked her loved ones for their kindness, then made her way around the room.

"He did well. You should be very proud." Lydia hugged Leah.

"Just a quick congrats hug! My girls are waiting in the car for me. They enjoyed the concert too, by the way!" Nicole hugged Leah as well.

"Thank you both so much for your kind words and yes, I am very proud!" Leah returned their acknowledgement.

Next, Leah went over to where Carolyn and the dance team had congregated. Carolyn commented, "The team wanted to stay because they knew JJ might sing. He was adorable! I'll wait outside with them until they've all been picked up."

"Thanks, Carolyn, I really appreciate your help. Thank you all for staying to watch JJ!"

The dancers huddled with Leah for one last group hug. Then, they each waved goodbye to Leah and left with Carolyn.

Debbie came up from behind, placed a hand on Leah's arm, then faced Leah for a hug. When Debbie stepped back, she exclaimed, "I can't believe it. He actually got on the stage and *sang*! Oh, he was so cute. He can sing!" Debbie had a surprised expression on her face. "I didn't know he could sing that well! He was so excited to tell me all about it. Love him!"

"Thanks, Debbie! I'm so glad you were able to see JJ sing."

"Me too. We're going to New York for school vacation week, which is actually this upcoming week. New York has a different school schedule than here in Massachusetts. Leah, your dancers…gorgeous! Your choreography…beautiful! Keep doing what you're doing. Love you!"

"Have fun in New York, and thank you! My dancers really made me proud, and that dance was definitely special. Love you too!" Leah hugged Debbie again.

JJ was laughing with Kay and Stef, who were the last people in the room. Leah put all their belongings in her bag and grabbed their coats. "Okay, JJ, we're ready to go. Kay, where did you park?"

"We're by the football field, because we know that's where you park too."

"Great! We can walk out together."

Kay and Stef each hugged Leah. "He was absolutely amazing!" Kay said to Leah.

"Yes, he is amazing. Right, JJ?" Stef agreed.

"Yay! I'm amazing!" JJ bounced as Leah tried to get his coat on.

"I love you both! Thanks again for staying with JJ today," Leah said to Kay and Stef.

Then, the family unit walked out of the school with light, carefree spirits.

Chapter Fourteen

Eric hoped Leah was home. Her car was in the driveway, and he hadn't seen her or JJ at the playground when he drove by. He took a deep breath, giving himself the strength he needed for what he anticipated would be a difficult conversation. He hoped…he wished to the clouds that floated in the sky, hoped that they could find a way to make it work, together. He tapped his phone to connect the call and closed his eyes, bringing the phone to his ear.

When her phone chimed, Leah wiggled herself free from under the blanket she shared with JJ as they snuggled on the couch. To not disturb him, she walked into the kitchen while she answered the call. "Hi, I was just thinking about you! JJ and I are watching *Toy Story*."

"That's fitting."

"Yeah, we're having a restful day after yesterday's exhilarating concert. Speaking of which, did your parents make it to the concert? I know you said that Ben was going to stay home with Madelyn to help her with the baby."

"Yes, my parents and Mrs. Dalton were there. They told me to tell you that they immensely enjoyed the entire concert, that your dance was lovely, and that JJ was 'darling,' my mom's words. They apologize that they didn't see you, but they wanted to get back to the baby."

"That's so sweet of them! Please thank them for me."

"Will do," he said. "Leah, can you please come downstairs for a few minutes, and would you mind not telling JJ that I'm here? I need to see you, if you think he will be okay by himself for a little while."

"Oh. I didn't realize that you were here." She looked out the window and saw Eric standing next to his car with a hand on his hip. "Are you okay?"

"I'm okay. I just need to see you...privately."

Something rolled in the pit of her stomach. Leah tried to push that feeling aside, wanting to believe that he only needed to see her because he missed her. "All right, then. Give me a minute to let JJ know that I'm going downstairs."

"Thank you." Eric disconnected the call and ran an unsteady hand through his hair.

When Leah opened the door, she and Eric exchanged a look of concern. "Come in," she offered, taking a moment to peer at the closed door before turning to face him. "I told JJ that I had something I needed to do in the studio. He's fine watching the movie by himself. What's going on, Eric?"

Eric tenderly held her hands, focusing on her graceful fingers. "I received a call from the University of Copenhagen. They want to publish my research papers."

"Oh, well, that sounds like a good thing. Congratulations, Eric!" Leah was cautiously optimistic, though his pensive mood worried her.

He looked into Leah's eyes, which had somewhat calmed. "Leah...they'll only publish my papers if I head their research department and work alongside their speech pathologists, physicians, and scientists."

Leah pulled her hands from his, blinking as tears began to blur her vision. "What are you saying, Eric?"

He put his hands in his pockets and stared down at his feet, then glanced back up at her eyes, which were no longer calm. "I have to move to Copenhagen."

Memories flooded her, and the room began to spin. Leah's knees couldn't support the weight that had just been dropped on her. She had to lean against the wall to keep herself upright, putting one hand to the gnawing roll in her stomach and the other to her pounding head.

This can't be happening, she thought. *Not again. He's leaving me.* She couldn't hold back the tears.

"I want to make this work for us, Leah." Eric reached out to wipe her tears, but she held up a hand, then wiped her face herself.

"How could it possibly work?" she asked. "Why do you have to go to Denmark? Did you try to find a publisher in Boston?"

"Immediately after you suggested it, I emailed the research departments at Harvard, Emerson, and Boston University with a link to my papers. I haven't heard from any of them and there's no guarantee that I will. As far as Copenhagen is concerned, their offer took me by surprise. It wasn't the position I had originally put in for. This offer will—"

Leah interrupted him, straightening to glare at him. "You applied for work in Copenhagen and never told me?"

"Before I met you, before I came here, I applied for a temporary professorship at the University of Copenhagen at the same time I applied to Bridge of Music, and sent along a copy of my papers. Lydia's offer came first. I never told you about Copenhagen because after I met you, after I fell for you, I knew that I wouldn't want a temporary professorship, and I honestly didn't think they would offer to publish my papers." He paused. "With the current offer, the university is interested in my therapeutic strategies and how they could be incorporated into their standards. My collaboration with them could lead to advancements in the field, additional resources for families, and the continued publication of my papers. This is what

I have worked so hard to achieve, and I did tell you that was my goal. Please know that this decision has not been easy for me."

"Does Lydia know?"

Eric shifted his weight and ran a hand through his hair. "Yes, she knows. Please, don't be upset with her. I asked her not to say anything to you. It needed to come from me. I didn't want anything to jeopardize JJ's chances of performing in the concert. When the—"

She interrupted him again. "You've known since before the concert?"

He lowered his head. "The call came on Friday, the day before the concert." He looked into Leah's distressed eyes. "Please know that I am not keeping anything from you. I would have told you that Friday if the concert hadn't been the next day."

Leah leaned her back against the wall again. There was a sharp ache in her chest, too close to her heart. "When...when are you leaving, Eric?" Her voice was quiet, struggling to speak through the pain.

With his hands on his hips, he turned away from her. After a long, deep breath, he faced her again, though she wouldn't look at him.

"This afternoon. My meeting with the research department is tomorrow."

Leah dropped her head into the palms of her hands. She couldn't breathe from the throbbing in her chest. The glimmer inside her, that had once been full and bright, dwindled.

Eric wanted so badly to hold her, to tell her that everything would be all right. Only, he didn't know how to make that happen. In his career, conflict and crisis resolution were his strengths, but in that moment, for the woman who meant the most to him, and for himself, he was at a loss.

He gave her a few minutes in silence, though the stillness in the air became too heavy. "Leah, please say something."

Continuing to lean against the wall, Leah crossed her arms over her chest, but did not make eye contact with him. "I can't ask you to stay," she said finally. "You've been offered your dream job, and I wish you success. You're amazing at what you do, and the university is fortunate to have you on their team. All I can say is that I've seen you with the kids from Bridge of Music, with JJ, and the impact you've made on their lives is significant. I've seen your passion for these kids, for my son, and I've seen your devotion to your family. My life, JJ's life, is here. My family, my friends, and my livelihood are all here. This is my home, where I belong, where I'm happy. You have…" Tears burned her eyes again and she fought to keep them away. "You have opened my heart and I let you in, when I didn't think I would ever be able to do so again. I thought you had found what you've been looking for in me. I guess I was wrong."

"Leah, you're not wrong. In you, I have found what I've been looking for. That's why I want us to find a way to make this work. Once I learn what my schedule will be like, I will fly back here as often as I can. Whenever JJ is not in school and you aren't teaching, both of you can fly to me. We can video call every day. I know it won't be easy or ideal, but we can make it work."

The tears fought their way out too quickly for Leah to catch them. While she rubbed the backs of her hands across her cheeks, she shook her head. "Eric, the fact would remain that we would be living in two different countries. I know there are couples who are happy with a life like that, and I applaud their strength, but I can't do it. My heart couldn't handle the separation, the loving visits, only to then have to say goodbye again, all the little daily moments that would be missed, the fear of you telling me that you are moving elsewhere again. I would wish for you to walk the journey with me, next to me, not an ocean away…but you would have to want that too. I can only tell you how I feel."

"Leah, I do want you," he said. "I wouldn't move anywhere else. I don't want you to fear that."

At that point, she looked at him. "That's exactly what you've been doing, though. For more than half your life, you've been traveling."

157

Frustrated with himself, Eric rubbed his chin and rocked his weight from one foot to the other. He didn't know why he couldn't find the right words. "I'm not giving up on us, Leah."

She walked past him to the stairs. "I can't talk about this anymore, Eric. It hurts too much. I need to get back to JJ." She stopped short. "Oh, JJ. He adores you. He's going to be devastated."

"Let me talk to him." He tried to follow her, but she turned toward him and held up a hand.

"No. Please, no."

"Okay." Eric backed up, then went to the door and looked at her one final time. "I will call you once I get to the airport. You're in my heart, Leah."

Then, he was gone. Leah's hand slid down the railing as her knees gave out. She sat on the stairs and wept.

* * *

Curled up in a corner of the couch, blanket up to her neck, Leah rested her head on the back of the couch and closed her eyes.

"Stef just texted me a picture of JJ on the swings. He looks like he's having fun." Kay tried to ease at least a small portion of Leah's distress.

"That's good. I'm glad she was able to get him out of the apartment. I didn't want him to see me like this."

With a comforting embrace, Kay sympathized, "I'm so, so sorry this has happened."

As Leah's vision glistened with tears, she pulled the sleep mask down over her eyes in an effort to escape from the pain, to lose herself in the darkness. "I don't know what to say to JJ. I have to tell him tonight, though, because, otherwise, he'll ask about the singing lesson he was supposed to have tomorrow."

"I guess just tell him the truth, but on a high level. He doesn't need to know the details," Kay suggested.

"Yeah."

When Leah's phone chimed, Kay recognized the caller. "Do you want to talk to Nicole?"

"You can answer it."

"Hey, Nicole, it's Kay...not so good...I'll let her know, thanks." Kay lifted the sleep mask off Leah's face. "Nicole and Lydia are on their way over."

As the light hit her, Leah squinted her eyes. "I'm not going to be good company."

"They know. Here, drink some water." Kay handed Leah the glass, then continued, "Last night, Stef made some chicken soup from Mom's recipe. I brought some for you and will heat up a bowl of it."

"I wish Mom and Daddy were here right now." Leah uncurled herself and sat upright for a sip of water.

"They are. You're going to get through this, Leah. They'll make sure of it. Love you."

"Love you too."

The sisters held each other tightly in an unconditional connection of their special bond, and Leah sighed into Kay's reassuring warmth. When Kay went into the kitchen, Leah noticed a droplet of water on the table in the shape of a heart. She circled a finger around it, and a small smile crept onto her face, bringing a moment of brightness to her eyes. "I love you too, Mom and Daddy."

By the time Nicole and Lydia arrived, Leah had finished a bowl of soup. She hadn't been hungry in the slightest, though she had humored her sister. It meant more to her that Kay and Stef were there with her and JJ.

"I come with chocolate," Nicole announced as she entered the kitchen. "Dark chocolate for you." She placed the bag on the table in front of Leah. "And M&M's for me. Of course, to share!" She bent down to hug Leah. "Lydia told me this morning. We wanted to come by and be with you. I'm going to put the kettle on the stove for some tea."

Leah opened the bag of her favorite sweet and unwrapped a bite-size piece. "Thanks, Nicole. I will definitely indulge today."

"Hello, dear." Lydia sat down next to Leah and placed her hand over Leah's with a gentle squeeze. "He asked me not to tell you. The timing may not have been ideal, but I do think he made the right decision to wait until after the concert to tell you. He was very concerned for JJ and you."

"Do you think his leaving is also the right decision?" Leah looked at Lydia with anguish in her eyes.

"Let me share this: when he told me, he was shaken. He was not the same confident man that he usually is."

Leah's phone chimed. When she saw that it was Eric, she turned the phone over. As the tears flowed, she looked back at Lydia. "Then why did he leave?"

"Sometimes, dear, it takes going to where you think you're supposed to be, in order to realize where it is that you're meant to be." Lydia squeezed Leah's hand again. "Try to believe in what your heart feels, dear."

* * *

Her home was quiet. Everyone had left, and JJ was in the shower. Leah was grateful for the support throughout the day, but she also needed time to herself.

After JJ was clean and had his pajamas on, Leah asked him for a snuggle on the couch before he went to bed.

"I love hugs!" he said.

"Me too, sweet face. And you give the best hugs!" While she held him, Leah propped her chin on the top of his freshly-shampooed head. "JJ, I have something to tell you." She paused to gather her strength then began, "Eric received an offer for a very important job. He will be working with scientists to find new ways of helping families and children like you and your friends at Bridge of Music.

But…" It hurt to think about it, never mind to say it. "The job is in Denmark, so he had to move there."

"Nooo!" JJ shook his head underneath hers. "That's all the way in Europe. I don't want him to go to Denmark."

"I know. I didn't want him to go, either."

"He already has an important job, Mommy. He teaches me and all the other kids."

"Yes, that's true, but he decided to change his job."

"Will he still be able to do singing lessons with me?"

"No, sweet face. He won't."

"I am too sad now, Mommy."

"I know. Me too."

They snuggled for a little while longer and Leah assured JJ that he would still have music class on Tuesday with Ms. Lydia and his friends. He said that he was too sad to sleep, but eventually, fatigue overcame him, and she was able to get him into bed. As she closed his door, Leah glanced at the tapestry on the wall, though its magical image now brought sorrow for her dreams that had suddenly disappeared.

Chapter Fifteen

"Bro, the sun has barely come up. Why are you calling so early?" Ben quickly ran into the kitchen so that he wouldn't wake up Madelyn.

"Sorry, I forgot about the time change. Did I wake anyone?"

"Yeah, me. I could've used those thirty minutes of sleep I still had left before my alarm went off!"

"Sorry, man. I don't know what's been wrong with me lately." Eric looked at his reflection in the hotel mirror. He had managed a few hours of sleep on the long flight and a few more once his head had hit the pillow at the hotel, though, jet lag and fatigue were not the cause of his unease and inability to focus. What was the cause? He scrutinized his reflection for an answer, though, he shook his head and rubbed the back of his neck when the reply was merely silence.

Ben heard the strain in his brother's voice, and that cleared the early morning fog from his head. "It's okay. I know this isn't easy for you. I'm sorry for flying off the handle like that. You made it to Copenhagen safely?"

"Yeah, I'm in the hotel. I need to jump in the shower and get to the university for my meeting. Ben, I can't get a hold of Leah. I've

162

left messages and texts, but she's not getting back to me. I can't lose her, but I'm afraid I already have."

"Eric, I think you need to give her some space. This can't be easy for her, either. Calling and texting her might be pushing her away. As hard as it will be, don't contact her for a while and give her time. If you really want, I can have Madelyn call her, although it's likely that Leah wouldn't pick up for Madelyn, because she'd know that Madelyn would be calling for you."

"Yeah, you're probably right. I'll lay off. Don't have Madelyn call her."

"I wish I could do more for you, big bro. Call me after your meeting?"

"Thanks for the advice, little bro. I hope you can catch a nap. I'll call you later."

* * *

Dressed in his finest, Eric waited in the university's office for his meeting. On his lap was a portfolio that held copies of his research papers and a blank pad for note-taking. Even though he'd never had an interview that involved his papers before, he knew his writings and could discuss his findings in his sleep.

He filled his wait time with photos on his phone. Warm memories played in his mind as he flipped through the pictures. His family, the wonder of the new life he held, the brotherly love he shared with Ben. Rehearsal with JJ, whose laughter was contagious, and whose outstanding bravery made him proud. He remembered the concert, all of his therapy clients and music students. The kids both motivated and moved him with their progress. He swiped to the next photo, the playground with JJ and Leah. He expanded the photo until Leah's face filled the screen, and he touched the image of her cheek. His mind flashed through all their moments together, linking their passionate and tender connection. Thoughts of her overflowed from his heart and found their way to the core of his soul. Leah's beauty stemmed from within, radiating through to her captivating outer features. She inspired him, ignited him. When he compressed the photo and took a good look at himself with JJ and Leah, he saw…

"Mr. Hynes?" A tall, professionally-clad woman stood in front of him.

Eric shoved his phone inside the pocket of his jacket, and stood with his portfolio in his arms. "Yes."

"Apologies for the wait. The team is ready for you now. I'll show you to the conference room. This way, please." She turned and led Eric down the hallway.

"Thank you very much. No apology necessary." Eric felt like himself again. He was ready, indeed.

* * *

Over the couple of days since Eric had gone, Leah was a shell of herself. Somehow, she made it through the days. She got JJ to and from school; she taught her dance classes. Though she smiled at her young dancers, listened to their stories, and made sure they had fun while they danced, she could no longer feel the music. At home, she comforted JJ when he became sad and missed Eric.

She cried in her private moments. Her heart ached for him. Eric had sent a flurry of messages within the initial few hours after he had left; Leah couldn't bring herself to read or listen to them, but she also didn't delete them. There hadn't been any new messages since then, which she convinced herself was a good thing, because she could move forward. *Well, maybe someday*, she thought. As of yet, she didn't want to extinguish the glimmer inside her, even though it was but a flicker on a wick.

JJ was "a little sad and a little happy," in his own words, when Leah dropped him off at Bridge of Music for his music class. As she locked the door to Dance World and headed back to Bridge of Music to pick him up, she shivered. The bitter cold had returned on that evening in early February, and she pulled her scarf up over her nose.

Snow was expected, though at that moment the velvety sky was peacefully still, illuminated by the white glow of the full moon.

When she walked through the doors to Bridge of Music, Leah hung her outerwear with JJ's on the coat rack and brushed the hair off her face that had clung from the static of her hat.

"Hi, Nicole." Leah leaned against Nicole's desk in the waiting area.

"How are you doing today?" Nicole stood and reached over the desk to hug Leah.

"I got through it the best I could. How are the girls?" Leah smiled at her childhood friend.

"Oh, you know them, different as can be!" Nicole laughed and rested her hands on her hips. "Lori will be doing a web design camp over school vacation, and Rebecca is in final rehearsals for the drama play."

Suddenly, the door to the music room flew open, and JJ bounded out. "Mr. Eric is back, Mommy! It's amazing!"

"What?" Leah looked at JJ, then to Nicole, who smiled brightly in return. She lost her balance as JJ collided with her in an exuberant embrace.

Two strong hands came to steady her shoulders. Leah lifted her head and looked up into the blue-gray eyes of the man who filled her heart. "What are you doing here?" she whispered in disbelief.

"I know what home means to me." Eric gently stroked her shoulders and became lost in the golden depths he had missed so terribly.

"What?"

Eric ruffled the hair of the young boy who still had his arms around Leah. "JJ, can you please go stand with Ms. Lydia? I need to talk to your mom."

"Okay, Mr. Eric!" JJ skipped over to Lydia and hugged her.

Eric brought his attention back to Leah, and chuckled. "It was four weeks ago to the day that I first laid eyes on you, Ms. Preston, Leah, and you looked at me then with the same dazed expression you're wearing now. Your sparkling golden eyes captivated me in that moment, and I have not been able to get you out of my head since." He brushed the flyaway strands of her hair behind her ear, caressing her cheek.

"But I thought you were in Copenhagen, that the university had offered you a position." Leah had longed for his touch, and the sensation of his skin clouded her thoughts.

"I was in Copenhagen, and their offer was everything I had been working to achieve professionally. Some things were missing, though. I turned them down."

"What? Why?"

"Well, for one thing, my family is here. I called Ben after my meeting to tell him I would be back, and he was thrilled. For another thing, the kids are here and, as you had said, I'm passionate about them, including JJ."

"Yay!" JJ bounced happily in Lydia's arms and everyone in the waiting area laughed. The other parents and children from the music class were on their feet, overjoyed to witness the romantic reunion playing out in front of them.

"I'm honored to announce that Lydia has graciously offered to transfer ownership of Bridge of Music to me. I am already beginning plans to expand the business to include field therapists, with the goal of transitioning the students from their homes to here at the studio, per Lydia's wishes. I applaud her years of commitment and wish her well in retirement." Eric clapped respectfully for her. The parents cheered, and the children rejoiced for both Lydia and Eric.

Leah went over to Lydia and hugged her tightly. "Congratulations! Thank you so much, for everything."

"Go back to him, dear. He has more to tell you." Lydia nudged Leah toward Eric.

When Leah again faced Eric, he held her hands and cupped her fingers in his. "When I was on my way back to the airport to return here, I received a call from Boston University. I met with their research department this morning. They'll be publishing my papers, and they've hired me as a consultant for their speech and language team."

"That's wonderful, Eric! It's what you've been wanting!"

Leah's eyes were shining at last, and Eric finally felt that he could smile from his heart. "There's one more thing that I want. You, Leah. I want you. When I was in Copenhagen, I felt afraid. You had once asked me what my biggest fear was, and I had said that I didn't have any. I would like to amend my reply. My biggest fear is losing you, and I was afraid that I had. Then, the universe knocked the sense back into me and told me that I was a fool for hurting you, for hurting JJ, for taking so long to see what had been in front of me all along and that I needed to make it right. I am immensely sorry and can only hope that you'll forgive me. Home, to me, means being with you and JJ." Eric looked lovingly at the young boy, who was the definition of joy.

"Amazing!" JJ bounced again, and his arms swung over his head in excitement.

Eric then looked deep into Leah's eyes and placed his heart in her hands. "I belong with you, Leah, next to you, for all the little moments, as well as the big ones. I don't want to travel anymore, unless it's with you by my side. I want to stay, with you…that is, if you'll have me. *Je t'aime*, Leah. I am truly, madly, deeply in love with you."

Leah blinked away her tears of happiness. As she stepped closer to him, she danced the backs of her fingers along his beard. With her signature sideways curve to her smile, she softly spoke, "So, you can speak with the universe, now?"

Eric smiled in return and rested his hands on her hips, his brow on hers. "Yes, yes I can. It's part of my qualifications as a speech and language pathologist."

She wrapped her arms around his neck. "Well, please tell the universe that I am eternally grateful it brought you back to me…and please have the universe remind you to never leave me again."

"It will never happen again. I promise."

"You are the music to my dance. *Je t'aime*, Eric. I am, with all of my heart and soul, in love with you."

Leah brushed her smile against his and when she parted her lips, he pulled her closer to him. As they melted into each other, all the spectators erupted with congratulatory applause.

"Hugs!" JJ ran over to Leah and Eric, wiggling his way in between them.

The glimmer inside her once again shimmered full and bright. Additionally, its glow held strength and tranquility. To the man who made her heart dance and to the boy who brought her heart joy, Leah said, "Let's go home."

Epilogue

L eah held her hand out in front of her again, admiring the rings on her finger. The satiny, oblong freshwater pearl had a string of small, clear diamonds angled across it, helping to hold it in its setting of alternating smaller diamonds and freshwater pearls, with a matching band. The rings' significance of a loving and committed unity held as much beauty, if not more, than the dazzling, ornate gems themselves.

Another year had passed, one that had been filled with new possibilities, successes, and true love. Another new year had just begun, with Leah's true love by her side. While a crystalline whiteness blanketed the outer surfaces on that Saturday afternoon in early January, almost one year to the day since they had met, she became his and he became hers, evermore. Leah floated in her euphoric state, an endless bliss written upon her face, highlighting her luminous golden eyes.

"They don't come close to the radiance of the woman wearing them." Her groom slid his hands around her waist from behind, brushed her hair off her shoulder, and nuzzled her neck. "Have I told you how beautiful you are?"

Leah affectionately rolled her thumb over the gold band on Eric's finger and reached her other arm around until her fingers tangled in his black locks. "Only about a dozen times."

"It bears repeating, Mrs. Preston-Hynes." Eric trailed his fingers up the cream-colored sheer fabric that covered Leah's arms, over the silky material encasing her shoulders, to the back of her neck and slowly unclasped the delicate buttons of her gown.

Momentarily lost in the tingling heat racing through her, Leah relaxed into his touch. Then, she remembered the hall filled with guests, just across the way from the small parlor they were in.

"No, no, button me back up!" she gasped, turning to face her handsome groom. There was a provocative look flowing in the waves of his sea.

"This isn't why you told me to meet you here?" Eric pulled her close to him, digging his fingers in her hips.

Leah spread her hands across his chest, then ran a graceful finger down the length of his dark gray tie, past his unbuttoned jacket, to the top of his pants. "That, my tempting husband, will have to wait until tonight, but I guarantee it will be worth the wait," she whispered, and looked up at him through lowered lashes.

Eric stole her lips in a kiss that filled her with the promise of passion and desire to come. When he reluctantly released her, he growled, in his deep raspy voice, clasping her gown back up, "You are something else."

She playfully laughed, then her expression changed to a loving warmth. "I have a surprise for you that'll be sure to please you, just in a very different way." Leah walked over to the garment bag for her gown and pulled out a manilla envelope. She hugged it to her, then handed it to Eric.

After he opened the envelope and pulled out the documents inside, he became emotional, processing the contents of the text. "Oh, my." The tears came fast. "It's official. I'm JJ's dad."

Leah wiped away her own tears, then his. "You have always been JJ's dad, in every way that matters. But yes, now it's official." She tenderly held Eric in her arms. "I love you so very much."

"I love you more." He closed his eyes and melted into her embrace.

About six months prior, just before the July Fourth holiday, Eric had taken Leah to his friend's French style café in Brookline and requested an intimate table for two in the back corner. After their meal, he had given her a gift: a small music box that played Debussy's "Clair de Lune." As Leah had wound the key and the romantic classical composition began, she had lifted the cover of the box and found a delicate ballerina figurine that slowly twirled. With the classical melody as the backdrop, Eric had moved center stage next to her and went down on one knee, opening an even smaller box to reveal the radiant ring Leah had been admiring just moments ago. His adoring words, of course, had brought tears of joy to her eyes. When she emphatically had said yes, Eric scooped her into his arms and spun her around.

After they had descended from the elation of Eric's romantic proposal, and before they had begun to discuss anything related to a wedding, the couple had decided that they would commence the process of a stepparent adoption for Eric and JJ. Because JJ's name would not be changed, however, Leah had planned to hyphenate her name, to honor both JJ and Eric.

"When did the documents come in?" Eric asked her, while he remained in her arms.

"Just yesterday. I wanted to surprise you with it today."

"Does JJ know?"

"Not yet. I'm thinking we can tell him together, after the two of you perform your song."

"That's perfect."

Leah thought that JJ was likely more excited for the wedding and adoption than she and Eric combined. He talked incessantly about it and counted down the days. Because he was driven by his excitement and anticipation, he had become more flexible in his behavior, and his anxiety has been better regulated; the morning of the wedding, he hadn't even noticed when Leah buttoned his blue collared shirt, or pulled up his dark gray dress pants. Though he didn't wear a jacket or tie, JJ was thrilled that he matched Eric's suit.

Additionally, when Eric had suggested to JJ that they should perform a song at the wedding, JJ had happily accepted, even though Eric had also told JJ that the lights would remain on. JJ had commented that he would be fine, because he would just be focused only on Eric during their song.

"We should go back into the hall with everyone. It's almost time for your song." Leah put the documents back inside the envelope. "Can you put this in your guitar case to keep it safe?"

"Will do."

They walked arm in arm into the main hall, where the reception was well under way. Eric kissed her cheek, then went off to set up for his song with JJ. Leah brimmed with happiness as she took in the celebratory atmosphere around her.

Nestled atop a hill at the end of the town's Main Street was the historic memorial hall named after a member of the affluent and influential family who resided in the town in the nineteenth century. Two renowned architects from that period had built the hall, from the grandiose outdoor staircase leading to multiple rounded arches, through which sat a covered terrace, opening into a spacious hall with a cathedral ceiling and elongated, stained-glass windows, to the detailed medieval artwork carved into the architecture. Outdoors, behind the historical grand structure, were artistically-landscaped gardens and streams. Such was the setting for Leah's and Eric's wedding.

Inside the hall, round tables were elegantly decorated with gray cotton tablecloths that draped to the floor, with an overlay of blue organza. The linen napkins were gold, the china white. Clear vases held white lilies in the center of each table.

Leah's gaze scanned the room to find her family as well as Eric's, her friends, her dance team, her village. She felt a renewed contentment that everyone was there for her for such a special occasion, solely for pure enjoyment. The band played lively music, and Leah's dance team made sure everyone was on the floor. Music, dance, and spirited voices filled the air; the ambience was palpable, so genuine.

Throughout the festivities, Leah had made her way to each table and spoke with or hugged everyone in attendance. Cameron, almost a year old, tried to pull himself up to his feet by holding onto a chair. Whenever Leah smiled and talked to him, he giggled and smiled in return, so much so that his pudgy arms went up in the air, which caused his padded bottom to drop to the floor when he released his grip on the chair. JJ found humor with Cameron and was proud to have a cousin. While Leah played with Cameron and JJ, Ben, who was Eric's best man, joined in to kiss Cameron's head and high five JJ. Suddenly, Ben swooped down to pull Leah up into his arms, as he then danced them into the center of the floor.

"Oh!" she exclaimed. Ben always seemed to take her by surprise. Her brother-in-law was definitely charming, but she knew he was quite devoted to his own wife.

"I needed to dance with my new sister. Maybe you can show me a move I can impress Madelyn with?" Ben twirled Leah, then pulled her back into his arms.

"I can show you a promenade pivot, if you don't already know that. Though, Ben, I believe you're all set when it comes to impressing Madelyn. All of you Hynes men are very charming, and Cameron is definitely following in your footsteps. He smiles at me every time I look at him, and he has my dancers in the palm of his little hand. They think he is adorable!"

"That's my boy!" Ben danced them closer to where Eric stood, talking with their parents. "Show me a promenade pivot."

"We start in an open position." She stepped back so their arms were extended. "Now, you lead by moving to your left, first with your left foot, then cross your right over your left. That's it. Now you step forward in front of me with your left foot and pull me closer to you by guiding your right hand against my back, and at the same time you pivot around with your right foot, then again with your left foot, so that we spin closely together. Now, we're back in the position where we started and further down the floor. Very good! Do you want to try it again?"

"Thanks, yeah. Let me see if I've got it."

Ben was a quick learner, she thought, as they pivoted down the floor again. "That was great, Ben! Madelyn will be impressed for sure."

"Excuse me, may I cut in please?" Eric was about to take Leah's hand when Ben twirled her away.

"Sorry big bro. I'm in the middle of a dance lesson."

Leah humorously shrugged her shoulders at Eric and blew him a kiss.

"Watch your hands, little bro!" Eric shouted over the music as Ben showed off his new move with Leah.

"I just like to give my brother a hard time." Ben laughed. "He's watching us like a hawk! Thank you for making my brother the happiest he's ever been, and thanks for the dance lesson too."

"He's made me the happiest I have ever been! And you're welcome for the lesson!"

As the song ended, Ben kissed Leah's hand. Then, he pulled Madelyn into his arms and onto the dance floor.

"May I please have this dance now?" Eric offered his hand to Leah, and she amorously went into his arms. He held her close as they became the rhythm of the music, with her hand by his heart and her head on his chest.

As Ben promenaded with Madelyn, Leah smiled. "Your brother wanted a new dance move to impress Madelyn with, so I taught him one. Looks like he and Madelyn are having a great time!"

"You'll have to show me some new dance moves."

"I will. Not now, though. I prefer yours." She sighed and closed her eyes, while he stroked her hair and leaned his head against hers.

When the song ended, Eric kissed her hair and breathed her in. Leah's scent was infused with that of the lilies in the whimsical wreath on her head. "I need to get JJ and prepare him for our song."

"I'm looking forward to it!"

Kay, Leah's matron of honor, in a flowing blue chiffon dress, came over to hug her sister. "You look very happy!"

"I'm extremely happy! Thank you for always being there for me. You look beautiful!"

"Love you!"

"I love you too! And thank you so much for letting JJ stay with you and Stef while I'm on my honeymoon. Paris! I can't believe I am actually going to Paris!"

"JJ will be fine. Make sure you send me lots of pictures!"

"I definitely will!"

The band announced that everyone needed to take their seats for a special performance. Leah hugged Kay, then made her way to where Eric and JJ were set up for their song. She stood just off to the side and watched with pride.

Eric sat with his guitar in his lap. JJ stood with his hands on Eric's shoulder. Eric turned his head to JJ and smiled as he began to strum their song. They had chosen "You'll Be in My Heart" from Disney's Tarzan. With their eyes connected, they sang and harmonized together. JJ didn't cover his ears or shade his eyes, nor did he hum. He sang the song in its entirety. They felt the music and brought the emotion of the lyrics to life. All in the room fell silent as the musical story reached the far corners of the hall and resonated into its high ceiling.

When everyone applauded, JJ then covered his ears and Eric stood to wrap an arm around JJ. At that point, Leah went over to them and hugged them each, then retrieved the documents from Eric's guitar case.

"JJ, we want to show you something." Leah held the documents so that JJ could see.

"What is this, Mommy?"

"These are the official documents for Eric's adoption of you," Leah explained.

Eric bent down to look into JJ's eyes. "JJ, I'm officially your dad. I love you, buddy."

"Yay! Amazing!" JJ wrapped himself around Eric, who lifted JJ off his feet and spun him around until they both were gleefully laughing. All the guests joined in with applause and cheers, some sighing for the sweetness of the revelation, others whistling for the achievement.

Once his feet were back on the floor, JJ opened one of his arms. "Group hug, Mommy!"

While Leah, JJ, and Eric were enclosed in an embrace, JJ looked at Leah then to Eric and rejoiced, "I love Mommy and Daddy!"

A quiet calmness swirled around Eric, and his heart was fulfilled. He had searched his whole life for what he, at that point, held in his arms. He ruffled JJ's hair as he looked at the young boy's beaming face. "My son." Then he looked at Leah, with her heartfelt smile and misty eyes. He touched the lilies in her hair and stroked her cheek. "My wife." He pulled both Leah and JJ close to him. "My family."

Leah kissed the top of JJ's head. "JJ, you are my miracle and my joy." She looked into Eric's eyes. His blue ocean was light. The waves were still, and softly flowed around the sea. She brushed the hair across his forehead. "Eric, you are my heart, my love, always."

Ben stood and raised a glass. "Here's to love in the new year!"

While all attendees acknowledged the toast, Leah and Eric, each with a hand on JJ's shoulders, sealed their love with a tender meeting of their lips.

Acknowledgements

To my sister, who reminded me how much I enjoy creative writing and encouraged me to write what I know. Thank you for going on this journey with me! I appreciate all your advice and support through all the texts, phone calls and emotional ups and downs. I love you!

To three of my longtime friends, who inspired me as I was developing characters. One friend, my best friend since childhood, with whom I am always at ease. Your strength is inspiring! No matter how long it may be between connections, we can always pick right up as if time has stood still. One friend who, when I walked into her dance studio (Dance Workshop in Easton, MA) as a young teen, saw something in me and made me part of her family. You changed my life for the better and have always been there for me professionally and personally. One friend who I met when our children bonded in preschool. You are a wealth of knowledge and a strong advocate in the world of those with disabilities. You embody the definition of inclusion! Thank you all for being the kind, understanding and accepting women you are! I am proud and honored that all of you are in my life!

To Karen Francioso-Howe, MS, CCC-SLP and Ashley Field, MS, CCC-SLP of Village Speech in North Easton, MA. Thank you both for your time and positive feedback regarding my portrayal of therapeutic interventions and of an SLP character. My son's years at Village Speech were extremely beneficial in his development, and I am beyond grateful for his speech and language therapists. The staff at Village Speech are warm, knowledgeable, supportive and strong advocates for those with disabilities!

To a very special speech and language pathologist with whom my son had the pleasure of working with when he was younger. You understood his needs and he made great progress with you! It was my honor to reconnect with you after all these years and to receive your valued feedback on my character's portrayal. I am grateful for your time and knowledge!

To Luke Moore, MT-BC of Glenville, New York. Thank you so much for your time and valued assistance regarding the musical aspects of my story and character portrayal of a music instructor! Luke is a coach and music teacher at a day program for adults with disabilities called LifeSong Inc. He is also a commhab worker for Resource Center for Independent Living. He just started his own business, Moore Excellent Way Music Therapy. Luke has a deep awareness of the needs of his clients and a passion for music. It was my pleasure to have been introduced to you, and I'm grateful for your knowledgeable and positive feedback!

To Dr. Li-Ching Wang, I am extremely grateful for your feedback on my SLP/music instructor character portrayal and the character's European experiences! Dr. Wang has a PhD degree in music psychology from University of Cambridge. She was a researcher in a music therapy center in London, doing research with music therapists and lecturing music therapy students. She is a music psychologist in New York. Your kindness, knowledge and experience are inspiring to me!

To Leah Romig, professional photographer in Easton, MA. Thank you for your time and patience in working with me. When I told you that I was used to being the one taking the pictures, not the one being photographed, you made me feel at ease, confident, and you brought out my personality. You went above and beyond for me, and your photos are beautiful!

To my neighbor, who is an established author herself, PK Norton (The Amy Lynch Investigations). Thank you for reading my story and recommending Stillwater River Publications. It means more than I can say that you were impressed with my story. Along with all your helpful suggestions, you have given me the confidence to move forward and achieve my writing goal! I am honored to be living next to you since before my son was even born!

To everyone at Stillwater River Publications, especially Steve and Dawn Porter, I extend heartfelt gratitude for all your guidance and assistance in making my book a reality! Sincere gratitude to the design team for the beautiful book cover! Thank you to the editing team, the printing team and all staff who have worked with my book on this journey! I am beyond grateful for your kindness and patience in helping me navigate the process as a first time author!

To my friends, my family and all of my son's teachers and therapists, thank you for being my village!

To my son, I love you with all my heart! You are amazing, and you spread joy to everyone! I'm proud of you and honored to be your mommy!

About the Author

Drawing on experiences from her life's journey, Lisa is delighted to share her first romance novel! Throughout her school years, she always enjoyed creative writing and hoped to one day write a story of her own. Her passion for dance from an early age led to her long career as a performer, choreographer and instructor. Her dance training during childhood began at The Gold School in Brockton, MA, then throughout her teens and beyond at Dance Workshop in Easton, MA. For several years as a young adult, she performed and assisted staging at Disney World Entertainment in FL. She was blessed to enter motherhood, in which she has walked through the door to the world of raising a child with a disability.

She is inspired by her son's love and abilities. She is grateful for her friends, family, all of her son's supportive team, and she makes an effort to give back. A hopeless romantic at heart and a loyal fan of Hallmark's romance movies, she is thrilled to achieve her writing goal in her novel, Love in the New Year!

Made in United States
North Haven, CT
05 February 2024

48358587R00104